CARSON (

Edgar Rice

C000242363

Foreword

India is a world unto itself, apart in manners, customs, occultism from the world and life with which we are familiar. Even upon far Barsoom or Amtor might be found no more baffling mysteries than those which lie hidden in the secret places of the brains and lives of her people. We sometimes feel that what we do not understand must be bad; that is our heritage from the ignorance and superstition of the painted savages from which we are descended. Of the many good things that have come to us out of India I am concerned at present with but one—the power which old Chand Kabi transmitted to the son of an English officer and his American wife to transmit his thoughts and visualizations to the mind of another at distances even as great as those which separate the planets. It is to this power we owe the fact that Carson Napier has been able to record, through me, the story of his adventures upon the planet Venus.

When he took off from Guadalupe Island in his giant rocket ship for Mars, I listened to the story of that epochal flight that ended, through an error in calculation, upon Venus. I followed his adventures there that started in the island kingdom of Vepaja where he fell desperately in love with Duare, the unattainable daughter of the king. I followed their wanderings across seas and land masses into the hostile city of Kapdor, and Kormor, the city of the dead, to glorious Havatoo, where Duare was condemned to death through a strange miscarriage of justice. I thrilled with excitement during their perilous escape in the aeroplane that Carson Napier had built at the request of the rulers of Havatoo. And always I suffered with Napier because of Duare's unalterable determination to look upon his love as an insult to the virgin daughter of the king of Vepaja. She repulsed him constantly because she was a princess, but in the end I rejoiced with him when she realized the truth and acknowledged that though she could not forget that she was a princess she had discovered that she was a woman first. That was immediately after they had escaped from Havatoo and were winging their way above the River of Death toward an unknown sea in seemingly hopeless search for Vepaja, where Duare's father, Mintep, ruled.

Months passed. I commenced to fear that Napier had crashed in his new ship, and then I began to have messages from him again which I shall record for the benefit of posterity as nearly in his own words as I can recall them.

2

I: DISASTER

Everyone who has ever flown will recall the thrill of his first flight over familiar terrain, viewing the old scenes from a new angle that imparted a strangeness and a mystery to them as of a new world; but always there was the comforting knowledge that the airport was not too far away and that even in the event of a forced landing one would know pretty well where he was and how to get home.

But that dawn that Duare and I took off from Havatoo to the accompaniment of the staccato hum of Amtorian rifles, I was actually flying over an unknown world; and there was no landing field and no home. I believe that this was the happiest and most thrilling moment of my life. The woman I love had just told me that she loved me, I was once again at the controls of a ship, I was free, I was flying in safety above the innumerable menaces that haunt the Amtorian scene. Undoubtedly, other dangers lay ahead of us in our seemingly hopeless quest for Vepaja, but for the moment there was nothing to mar our happiness or arouse forebodings. At least, not in me. With Duare it may have been a little different. She may have had forebodings of disaster. It would not be strange if she had, for up until the very instant that we rose to top the walls of Havatoo she had had no conception that there might exist any contrivance in which man might leave the ground and fly through the air. It was naturally something of a shock to her; but she was very brave, and content, too, to accept my word that we were safe.

The ship was a model of perfection, such a ship as will one day be common along the airways of old Earth when science has progressed there as far as it has in Havatoo. Synthetic materials of extreme strength and lightness entered into her construction. The scientists of Havatoo assured me that she would have a life of at least fifty years without overhaul or repairs other than what might be required because of accident. The engine was noiseless and efficient beyond the dreams of Earth men. Fuel for the life of the ship was aboard; and it took up very little space, for it could all be held in the palm of one hand. This apparent miracle is scientifically simple of explanation. Our own scientists are aware of the fact that the energy released by combustion is only an infinitesimal fraction of that which might be generated by the total annihilation of a substance. In the case of coal it is as eighteen thousand millions are to one. The fuel for my engine consists of a substance known as *lor*, which contains an element called *yor-san*, as yet unknown to Earth men, and another element, *vik-ro*, the action of which upon *yor-san* results in absolute annihilation of the *lor*.

Insofar as the operation of the ship was concerned, we might have flown on for fifty years, barring adverse weather conditions; but our weakness lay in the fact that we had no provisions. The precipitancy of our departure had precluded any possibility of provisioning the ship. We had escaped with our lives and what we had on, and that was all; but we were very happy. I didn't want to spoil it by questioning the future. But, really, we had a great many questions to ask of the future; and Duare presently raised one quite innocently enough.

"Where are we going?" she asked.

"To look for Vepaja," I told her. "I am going to try to take you home."

She shook her head. "No, we can't go there."

"But that is the one place you have been longing to go ever since you were kidnaped by the klangan," I reminded her.

"But not now, Carson. My father, the jong, would have you destroyed. We have spoken of love to one another, and no man may speak of love to the daughter of the jong of Vepaja before she is twenty. You know that well enough."

"I certainly should," I teased her; "you have told me often enough."

"I did it for your own safety, but nevertheless I always liked to hear you say it," she admitted.

"From the first?" I asked.

"From the first. I have loved you from the first, Carson."

"You are an adept at dissimulation. I thought you hated me; and yet, sometimes I wondered."

"And because I love you, you must never fall into the hands of my father."

"But where can we go, Duare? Do you know a single spot in all this world where we should be safe? There is none; and in Vepaja you, at least, will be safe. I shall have to take the chance of winning your father over."

"It could never be done," she declared. "The unwritten law that decrees this thing is as old as the ancient empire of Vepaja. You have told me of the gods and goddesses of the religions of your world. In Vepaja the royal family occupies a similar position in the minds and hearts of the people, and this is especially true of the virgin daughter of a jong—she is absolutely sacrosanct. To look at her is an offense; to speak to her is a crime punishable by death."

"It's a crazy law," I snapped. "Where would you be now, had I abided by its dictates?—dead. I should think your father would feel some obligation toward me."

"As a father, he would; but not as a jong."

4

"And I suppose he is a jong first," I said, a little bitterly.

"Yes, he is a jong first; and so we may not return to Vepaja," she said with finality.

What an ironical trick Fate had played upon me. With many opportunities in two worlds to pick a girl for me to fall in love with, she had ended up by choosing a goddess. It was tough, yet I wouldn't have had it otherwise. To have loved Duare, and to know that she loved me, was better than a lifetime with any other woman.

Duare's decision that we must not return to Vepaja had left me in something of a quandary. Of course I didn't know that I could have found Vepaja anyway, but at least it was something to aim at. Now I had nothing. Havatoo was the grandest city I had ever seen; but the unbelievable decision of the judges who had examined Duare after I had rescued her from the City of the Dead, and our escape, made it impossible for us ever to return. To hunt for a hospitable city in this strange world seemed useless and hopeless. Venus is a world of contradictions, anomalies, and paradoxes. In the midst of scenes of peace and beauty, one meets the most fearsome beasts; among a friendly, cultured people exist senseless and barbarous customs; in a city peopled by men and women of super-intelligence and sweetness the quality of mercy is utterly unknown to its tribunals. What hope had I, then, of finding a safe retreat for Duare and myself? I determined then to return Duare to Vepaja, that she, at least, might be saved.

We were flying south along the course of Gerlat kum Rov, The River of Death, toward the sea to which I knew the waters must eventually guide me. I was flying low, as both Duare and I wished to see the country rolling majestically beneath us. There were forests and hills and plains and, in the distance, mountains; while over all, like the roof of a colossal tent, stretched the inner cloud envelope that entirely surrounds the planet; and which, with the outer cloud bank, tempers the heat of the sun and makes life possible on Venus. We saw herds of animals grazing on the plains, but we saw no cities and no men. It was a vast wilderness that stretched below us, beautiful but deadly—typically Amtorian.

Our course was due south, and I believed that when we reached the sea we would but have to continue on across it to find Vepaja. Knowing that Vepaja was an island, and always having in mind that some day I might wish to return to it, I had designed my ship with retractable pontoons as well as ordinary landing gear.

The sight of the herds below us suggested food and stimulated my appetite. I asked Duare if she were hungry. She said she was—very—but asked what good it would do her.

"There's our dinner down there," I said, pointing.

"Yes, but by the time we get down there it will be gone," she said. "Wait till they catch a glimpse of this thing. There won't be one of them within miles by the time you get this thing on the ground—unless it scares some of them to death."

She didn't say miles, of course; she said *klookob*, *kob* being a unit of distance equivalent to 2.5 earth miles, the prefix *kloo* denoting the plural. But she did say 'this thing' in Amtorian.

"Please don't call my beautiful ship 'this thing,'" I begged.

"But it is not a ship," she demurred. "A ship goes on water. I have a name for it, Carson—it is an *anotar*."

"Splendid!" I applauded. "*Anotar* it shall be."

It was a good name, too; for *notar* means ship, and an is the Amtorian word for bird—birdship. I thought this better than airship, possibly because Duare had coined it.

I had an elevation of about a thousand feet; but as my motor was absolutely noiseless, none of the animals beneath us was yet aware of the strange thing hovering above them. As I started to spiral downward, Duare gave a little gasp and touched my arm. She didn't seize it, as some women might have; she just touched it, as though the contact gave her assurance. It must have been rather a terrifying experience for one who had never even seen an airship before that morning.

"What are you going to do?" she asked.

"I'm going down after our dinner. Don't be frightened."

She said no more, but she still kept her hand on my arm. We were dropping rapidly when suddenly one of the grazing animals looked up; and, at sight of us, gave a loud snort of warning and went careening off across the plain. Then they all stampeded. I straightened out and went after them, dropping down until I was just above their backs. At the altitude at which we had been flying, the ground speed had probably seemed slow to her; so that now that we were but a few feet above ground it surprised her to find that we could easily outdistance the fleetest of the racing beasts.

I do not consider that it is very sporting to shoot animals from an airplane, but I was not indulging in sport—I was after food, and this was about the only way that I could get it without endangering our lives by stalking on foot; so it was without compunction that I drew my pistol and brought down a fat young yearling of some strange herbivorous species unknown to our world; at least, I guess it was a yearling—it looked as though it should be. The chase had brought us quite close to a fringe of forest that grew along the banks of a tributary of the River of Death; so that I had to bank quite sharply to avoid piling up among the trees. When I glanced at Duare she was quite white, but she was keeping a stiff upper lip. By the time I landed beside my kill, the plain was deserted.

Leaving Duare in the cockpit, I got out to bleed and butcher the animal. It was my intention to cut off as much meat as I thought would remain fresh until we could use it and then take off and fly to a more suitable temporary campsite.

I was working close beside the plane, and neither Duare nor I faced the forest which lay but a short distance behind us. Of course, we were careless in not maintaining a better watch; but I suppose we were both intent on my butchering operations, which, I must admit, were doubtless strange and wonderful to behold.

The first intimation I had of impending danger was a frightened cry of "Carson!" from Duare. As I wheeled toward her, I saw fully a dozen warriors coming for me. Three of them were right on top of me with raised swords. I saw no chance of defending myself; and went down beneath those swords like a felled ox, but not before the brief glimpse I had of my attackers revealed the astonishing fact that they were all women.

I must have lain there unconscious for more than an hour, and when I regained consciousness I found myself alone—the warriors and Duare were gone.

II: WARRIOR WOMEN

I came at that moment to being as nearly spiritually crushed as I ever had been before in my life. To have Duare and happiness snatched from me after a few brief hours, at the very threshold of comparative security, completely unnerved me for the moment. It was the more serious aspect of the situation that gave me control of myself once more—the fate of Duare.

I was pretty badly mussed up. My head and the upper part of my body were caked with dried blood from several nasty sword cuts. Why I had not been killed I shall never understand, and I am certain that my attackers had left me for dead. My wounds were quite severe, but none of them was lethal. My skull was intact; but my head ached frightfully, and I was weak from shock and loss of blood.

An examination of the ship showed that it had not been damaged or tampered with; and as I glanced around the plain I saw that which convinced me that its presence there had doubtless saved my life, for there were several savage-appearing beasts pacing to and fro some hundred yards away eyeing me hungrily. It must have been the, to them, strange monster standing guard over me that kept them at bay.

The brief glimpse I had had of the warrior women suggested that they were not mere savages but had attained at least some degree of civilization—their apparel and arms bespoke that. From this I assumed that they must live in a village; and as they were on foot, it was reasonable to suppose that their village was at no great distance. I was sure that they must have come out of the forest behind the ship and therefore that it was in this direction I must search for Duare first.

We had seen no village before landing, as it seemed almost certain that we should have had one of any size existed within a few miles of our position, for both of us had been constantly on the lookout for signs of the presence of human beings. To prosecute my search on foot, especially in view of the presence of the savage carnivores hungrily anticipating me, would have been the height of foolishness; and if the village of the warrior women were in the open I could find it more quickly and more easily from the plane.

I was rather weak and dizzy as I took my place at the controls, and only such an emergency as now confronted me could have forced me into the air in the condition in which I was. However, I made a satisfactory take-off; and once in the air my mind was so occupied by my search that I almost forgot my hurts. I flew low over the forest and as silently as a bird on the wing. If there were a village and if it were built in the forest, it might be difficult or even impossible to locate it from the air, but because of the

8

noiselessness of my ship it might be possible to locate a village by sound could I fly low enough.

The forest was not of great extent; and I soon spanned it, but I saw no village nor any sign of one. Beyond the forest was a range of hills, and through a pass in them I saw a well worn trail. This I followed; but I saw no village, though the landscape lay spread before me for miles around. The hills were cut with little canyons and valleys. It was rough country where one would least expect to find a village; and so I gave up the search in this direction and turned the nose of my ship back toward the plain where Duare had been captured, intending to start my search from there in another direction.

I was still flying very low, covering once more the ground I had just been over, when my attention was attracted by the figure of a human being walking rapidly across a level mesa. Dropping still lower, I saw that it was a man. He was walking very rapidly and constantly casting glances behind. He had not discovered the ship. Evidently he was too much concerned with whatever was behind him, and presently I saw what it was—one of those ferocious lion-like creatures of Amtor, a tharban. The beast was stalking him; but I knew that it would soon charge, and so I dropped quickly in a steep dive. Nor was I a moment too soon.

As the beast charged, the man turned to face it with his pitifully inadequate spear, for he must have known that flight was futile. I had drawn my Amtorian pistol, charged with its deadly r-ray; and as I flattened out just above the tharban, narrowly missing a crack-up, I let him have it. I think it was more luck than skill that permitted me to hit him at all; and as he rolled over and over on the ground, I banked, circled the man and made a landing behind him. He was the first human being I had seen since the capture of Duare, and I wanted to question him. He was alone, armed only with primitive weapons; and, so, absolutely in my power.

I don't know why he didn't run away; for that airship must have been an appalling thing to him; but he stood his ground even as I taxied up and stopped near him. It may have been that he was just paralyzed by fright. He was a small, rather insignificant looking fellow wearing a loincloth so voluminous as to appear almost a short skirt. About his throat were several necklaces of colored stones and beads, while armlets, bracelets, and anklets similarly fabricated adorned his limbs. His long black hair was coiled in two knots, one upon either temple; and these were ornamented with tiny, colored feathers stuck into them like arrows in a target. He carried a sword, a spear, and a hunting knife.

As I descended from the ship and approached him, he backed away; and his spear arm started back menacingly. "Who are you?" he asked. "I don't want to kill you, but if you come any closer I'll have to. What do you want?"

9

"I don't want to harm you," I assured him; "I just want to talk to you." We spoke in the universal language of Amtor.

"What do you want to talk to me about?—but first tell me why you killed the tharban that was about to kill and eat me?"

"So that it wouldn't kill and eat you."

He shook his head. "That is strange. You do not know me; we are not friends; so why should you wish to save my life?"

"Because we are both men," I told him.

"That is a good idea," he admitted. "If all men felt that way we would be treated better than we are. But even then, many of us would be afraid. What is that thing you were riding in? I can see now that it is not alive. Why does it not fall to the ground and kill you?"

I had neither the time nor inclination to explain the science of aerodromics to him; so I told him it stayed up because I made it stay up.

"You must be a very wonderful man," he said admiringly. "What is your name?"

"Carson—and yours?"

"Lula," he replied, and then, "Carson is a strange name for a man. It sounds more like a woman's name."

"More so than Lula?" I asked, restraining a smile.

"Oh, my, yes; Lula is a very masculine name. I think it is a very sweet name, too; don't you?"

"Very," I assured him. "Where do you live, Lula?"

He pointed in the direction from which I had just come after abandoning hope of finding a village there. "I live in the village of Houtomai that is in The Narrow Canyon."

"How far is it?"

"About two *klookob*," he estimated.

Two *klookob!* That would be five miles of our system of linear measurement, and I had flown back and forth over that area repeatedly and hadn't seen any sign of a village.

"A little while ago I saw a band of warrior women with swords and spears," I said. "Do you know where they live?"

"They might live in Houtomai," he said, "or in one of several other villages. Oh, we Samary have many villages; we are very powerful. Was one of the women large and powerful and with a deep scar on the left side of her face?"

"I really didn't have much opportunity to observe them closely," I told him.

"Well, perhaps not. If you'd gotten too close to them you'd be dead now, but I thought maybe Bund might have been with them; then I would have known that they were from Houtomai. Bund, you see, is my mate. She is very strong, and really should be chief." He said *jong*, which means king; but chief seems a better title for the leader of a savage tribe, and from my brief intercourse with the ladies of the Samary I could vouch for their savagery.

"Will you take me to Houtomai?" I asked.

"Oh, mercy, no," he cried. "They'd kill you, and after your having saved my life I couldn't think of exposing you to danger."

"Why would they want to kill me?" I demanded. "I never did anything to them and don't intend to."

"That doesn't mean anything to the women of the Samary," he assured me. "They don't like men very well, and they kill every strange man they find in our country. They'd kill us, too, if they weren't afraid the tribe would become extinct. They do kill some of us occasionally, if they get mad enough. Bund tried to kill me yesterday, but I could run too fast for her. I got away, and I've been hiding out since. I think perhaps she's gotten over her anger by now; so I'm going to sneak back and see."

"Suppose they captured a strange woman," I asked, "what would they do with her?"

"They'd make a slave of her and make her work for them."

"Would they treat her well?"

"They don't treat anyone well—except themselves; they live on the fat of the land," he said, resentfully.

"But they wouldn't kill her?" I asked. "You don't think they'd do that, do you?"

He shrugged. "They might. Their tempers are very short; and if a slave makes a mistake, she'd certainly be beaten. Often they beat them to death."

"Are you very fond of Bund?" I asked him.

"Fond of Bund! Who ever heard of a man being fond of a woman? I hate her. I hate them all. But what can I do about it? I must live. If I went to another country, I'd be killed. If I stay here and try to please Bund, I am fed and protected and have a place to sleep. And then, too, we men do have a little fun once in a while. We can sit around and talk while we're making sandals and loincloths, and sometimes we play games—that is, when the women are out hunting or raiding. Oh, it's better than being dead, anyhow."

"I'm in trouble, Lula; and I'm wondering if you won't help me. You know we men should stick together."

"What do you want me to do?" he demanded.

"I want you to lead me to the village of Houtomai."

He looked at me suspiciously, and hesitated.

"Don't forget that I saved your life," I reminded him.

"That's right," he said. "I do owe you something—a debt of gratitude, at least. But why do you want to go to Houtomai?"

"I want to see if my mate is there. She was stolen by some warrior women this morning."

"Well, why do you want to get her back? I wish some one would steal Bund."

"You wouldn't understand, Lula," I told him; "but I certainly do want to get her back. Will you help me?"

"I could take you as far as the mouth of The Narrow Canyon," he said; "but I couldn't take you into the village. They'd kill us both. They'll kill you when you get there, anyway. If you had black hair you might escape notice, but that funny yellow hair of yours would give you away the very first thing. Now, if you had black hair, you could sneak in after dark and come into one of the men's caves. That way you might escape notice for a long time. Even if some of the women saw you, they wouldn't know the difference. They don't pay much attention to any but their own men."

"But wouldn't the men give me away?"

"No; they'd think it was a great joke—fooling the women. If you were found out, we'd just say you fooled us, too. My, I wish you had black hair."

I, too, wished then that I had black hair, if that would help me get into the village of Houtomai. Presently, a plan occurred to me.

"Lula," I asked, "did you ever see an *anotar* before?" nodding toward the ship.

He shook his head. "Never."

"Want to have a look at it?"

He said he'd like to; so I climbed into the cockpit, inviting him to follow me. When he had seated himself beside me, I buckled the safety belt across him to demonstrate it as I was explaining its purpose.

"Would you like to take a ride?" I asked.

"Up in the air?" he demanded. "Mercy, I should say not."

"Well, just along the ground, then."

"Just a little way along the ground?"

"Yes," I promised, "just a little way along the ground," and I wasn't lying to him. I taxied around until we were headed into the wind; then I gave her the gun.

"Not so fast!" he screamed; and he tried to jump out, but he didn't know how to unfasten the safety belt. He was so busy with it that he didn't look up for several seconds. When he did, we were a hundred feet off the ground and climbing rapidly. He gave one look, screamed, and closed his eyes. "You lied to me," he cried. "You said we'd go just a little way along the ground."

"We ran only a little way along the ground," I insisted. "I didn't promise that I wouldn't go into the air." It was a cheap trick, I'll admit; but there was more than life at stake for me, and I knew that the fellow was perfectly safe. "You needn't be afraid," I reassured him. "It's perfectly safe. I've flown millions of *klookob* in perfect safety. Open your eyes and look around. You'll get used to it in a minute or two, and then you'll like it."

He did as I bid, and though he gasped a bit at first he soon became interested and was craning his neck in all directions looking for familiar landmarks.

"You're safer here than you would be on the ground," I told him; "neither the women nor the tharbans can get you."

"That's right," he admitted.

"And you should be very proud, too, Lula."

"Why?" he demanded.

"As far as I know, you're the third human being ever to fly in the air in Amtor, excepting the klangan; and I don't count them as human, anyway."

13

"No," he said, "they're not—they're birds that can talk. Where are you taking me?"

"We're there. I'm coming down now." I was circling above the plain where I had made the kill before Duare was stolen. A couple of beasts were feeding on the carcass, but they took fright and ran away as the ship dropped near them for a landing. Jumping out, I cut strips of fat from the carcass, threw them into the cockpit, climbed in and took off. By this time, Lula was an enthusiastic aeronaut, and if it hadn't been for the safety belt he would have fallen out in one of his enthusiastic attempts to see everything in all directions at one and the same time. Suddenly, he realized that we were not flying in the direction of Houtomai.

"Hey!" he cried. "You're going in the wrong direction—Houtomai is over there. Where are you going?"

"I'm going to get black hair," I told him.

He gave me a frightened look. I guess he thought he was up in the air with a maniac; then he subsided, but he kept watching me out of the corner of an eye.

I flew back to The River of Death, where I recalled having seen a low, flat island; and, dropping my pontoons, landed on the water and taxied into a little cove that indented the island. I managed, after a little maneuvering, to get ashore with a rope and tie the ship to a small tree; then I got Lula to come ashore and build me a fire. I could have done it myself, but these primitive men accomplish it with far greater celerity than I ever could acquire. From a bush I gathered a number of large, waxlike leaves. When the fire was burning well, I took most of the fat and dropped it in piece by piece and very laboriously and slowly accumulated soot on the waxy faces of the leaves. It took much longer than I had hoped it would, but at last I had enough for my purpose. Mixing the soot with a small quantity of the remaining fat I rubbed it thoroughly into my hair, while Lula watched me with a broadening grin. From time to time I used the still surface of the cove for a mirror, and when I had completed the transformation I washed the soot from my hands and face, using the ashes of the fire to furnish the necessary lye to cut the greasy mess. At the same time, I washed the blood from my face and body. Now I not only looked, but felt, like a new man. I was rather amazed to realize that during all the excitement of the day I had almost forgotten my wounds.

"Now, Lula," I said, "climb aboard and we'll see if we can find Houtomai."

The take-off from the river was rather exciting for the Amtorian, as I had to make a very long run of it because of the smoothness of the water, throwing spray in all directions; but at last we were in the air and headed for Houtomai. We had a little difficulty in locating The Narrow Canyon because from this new vantage point the ordinarily familiar terrain took on a new aspect for Lula, but at last he gave a yell and pointed down. I looked and saw a narrow canyon with steep walls, but I saw no village.

14

"Where's the village?" I asked.

"Right there," replied Lula, but still I could not see it; "but you can't see the caves very well from here."

Then I understood—Houtomai was a village of cave dwellers. No wonder I had flown over it many times without recognizing it. I circled several times studying the terrain carefully, and also watching the time. I knew that it must be quite close to sundown, and I had a plan. I wanted Lula to go into the canyon with me and show me the cave in which he dwelt. Alone, I could never have found it. I was afraid that if I brought him to the ground too soon he might take it into his head to leave for home at once; then there would have been trouble, and I might have lost his help and cooperation.

I had found what I considered a relatively safe place to leave the ship, and as night was falling I brought her into a beautiful landing. Taxiing to a group of trees, I tied her down as best I could; but I certainly hated to go off and leave that beautiful thing alone in this savage country. I was not much concerned for fear that any beast would damage it. I was sure they would be too much afraid of it to go near it for a long while, but I didn't know what some ignorant human savages might do to it if they found it there. However, there was nothing else to be done.

Lula and I reached The Narrow Canyon well after dark. It was not a very pleasant trip, what with savage hunting beasts roaring and growling in all directions and Lula trying to elude me. He was commencing to regret his rash promises of help and think of what would certainly happen to him if it were discovered that he had brought a strange man into the village. I had to keep constantly reassuring him that I would protect him and swear by all that an Amtorian holds holy that I had never seen him, in the event that I should be questioned by the women.

We reached the foot of the cliff, in which the caves of the Houtamaians were carved, without exciting incident. Some fires were burning on the ground—two fires, a large one and a small one. Around the large fire were grouped a number of strapping women, squatting, lying, standing. They shouted and laughed in loud tones as they tore at pieces of some animal that had been cooking over the fire. Around the smaller fire sat a few little men. They were very quiet; and when they spoke, it was in low tones. Occasionally, one of them would giggle; and then they would all look apprehensively in the direction of the women, but the latter paid no more attention to them than as though they had been so many guinea pigs.

To this group of men, Lula led me. "Say nothing," he warned his unwelcome guest, "and try not to call attention to yourself."

I kept to the rear of those gathered about the fire, seeking always to keep my face in shadow. I heard the men greet Lula, and from their manner I judged that a bond of

15

friendship, welded from their common misery and degradation, united them. I looked about in search of Duare, but saw nothing of her.

"How is Bund's humor," I heard Lula inquire.

"As bad as ever," replied one of the men.

"Were the raids and the hunting good today? Did you hear any of the women say?" continued Lula.

"They were good," came the reply. "There is plenty of meat now, and Bund brought in a woman slave that she captured. There was a man with her, whom they killed, and the strangest contraption that anyone ever beheld. I think even the women were a little afraid of it from what they said. At any rate, they evidently got away from it as quickly as they could."

"Oh, I know what that was," said Lula; "it was an anotar."

"How do you know what it was?" demanded one of the men.

"Why—er—can't you take a joke?" demanded Lula in a weak voice.

I smiled as I realized how nearly Lula's vanity had caused him to betray himself. It was evident that while he may have trusted his friends, he did not therefore trust them implicitly. And I smiled also from relief, for I knew now that I had come to the right village and that Duare was here—but where? I wanted to question these men, but if Lula could not trust them, how might I? I wanted to stand up and shout Duare's name. I wanted her to know that I was here, eager to serve her. She must think me dead; and, knowing Duare as I did, I knew that she might take her own life because of hopelessness and despair. I must get word to her somehow. I edged toward Lula, and when I was close to him whispered in his ear.

"Come away. I want to talk to you," I said.

"Go away. I don't know you," whispered Lula.

"You bet you know me; and if you don't come with me, I'll tell 'em all where you've been all afternoon and that you brought me here."

"Oh, you wouldn't do that!" Lula was trembling.

"Then come with me."

"All right," said Lula, and rising walked off into the shadows beyond the fire.

I pointed toward the women. "Is Bund there?" I asked.

"Yes, the big brute with her back toward us," replied Lula.

"Would her new slave be in Bund's cave?"

"Probably."

"Alone?" I asked.

"No, another slave whom Bund could trust would be watching her, so that she couldn't escape."

"Where is Bund's cave?"

"High up, on the third terrace."

"Take me to it," I directed.

"Are you crazy, or do you think I am?" demanded Lula.

"You are allowed on the cliff, aren't you?"

"Yes, but I wouldn't go to Bund's cave unless she sent for me."

"You don't have to go there; just come with me far enough to point it out to me."

He hesitated, scratching his head. "Well," he said, finally, "that's as good a way as any to get rid of you; but don't forget that you promised not to tell them that it was I who brought you to the village."

I followed him up a rickety ladder to the first and then to the second level, but as we were about to ascend to the third two women started down from above. Lula became panicky.

"Come!" he whispered nervously and took me by the arm.

He led me along a precarious footwalk that ran in front of the caves and to the far end of it. Trembling, he halted here.

"That was a narrow escape," he whispered. "Even with your black hair you don't look much like a Samaryan man—you're as big and strong as a woman; and that thing hanging at your side—that would give you away. No one else has one. You'd better throw it away."

He referred to my pistol, the only weapon I had brought, with the exception of a good hunting knife. The suggestion was as bizarre as Lula was naive. He was right in saying

17

that its possession might reveal my imposture, but on the other hand its absence might insure my early demise. I did manage to arrange it, however, so that it was pretty well covered by my loincloth.

As we were standing on the runway waiting for the two women to get safely out of the way, I looked down upon the scene below, my interest centering principally upon the group of women surrounding the larger fire. They were strapping specimens, broad shouldered, deep chested, with the sturdy limbs of gladiators. Their hoarse voices rose in laughter, profanity, and coarse jokes. The firelight played upon their almost naked bodies and their rugged, masculine faces, revealing them distinctly to me. They were not unhandsome, with their short hair and bronzed skins; but even though their figures were, in a modified way, those of women, there seemed not even a trace of femininity among them. One just could not think of them as women, and that was all there was to it. As I watched them, two of them got into an altercation. They started by calling each other vile names; then they went at it hammer and tongs, and they didn't fight like women. There was no hair pulling or scratching there. They fought like a couple of icemen.

How different the other group around the smaller fire. With mouselike timidity they furtively watched the fight—from a distance. Compared with their women, their bodies were small and frail, their voices soft, their manner apologetic.

Lula and I didn't wait to ascertain the outcome of the fight. The two women who had interrupted our ascent passed down to a lower level leaving us free to climb to the next runway where Bund's cave was located. When we stood upon the catwalk of the third level, Lula told me that Bund's cave was the third to my left. That done, he was ready to leave me.

"Where are the men's caves?" I asked him before he could get away.

"On the highest level."

"And yours?"

"The last cave to the left of the ladder," he said. "I'm going there now. I hope I never see you again." His voice was shaking and he was trembling like a leaf. It didn't seem possible that a man could be reduced to such a pitiable state of abject terror, and by a woman. Yet he had faced the tharban with a real show of courage. With a shake of my head I turned toward the cave of Bund, the warrior woman of Houtomai.

III: CAVES OF HOUTOMAI

The catwalks before the caves of the cliff dwellers of Houtomai seemed most inadequate; but they served their purpose, and I suppose the dwellers there, being accustomed to nothing different, were content with them. Their construction was simple but practical. Into holes bored in the face of the sandstone cliff, straight tree limbs had been driven projecting about two feet from the cliff. These were braced by other pieces, the lower ends of which rested in notches cut about two feet below the holes. Along the tops of these brackets, poles had been laid and lashed down with rawhide. The runways seemed rather narrow when one glanced down the face of the precipitous cliff, and there were no handrails. I couldn't help but think how embarrassing it might be to get into a fight on one of these catwalks. As these thoughts passed through my mind, I made my way to the mouth of the third cave to my left. All as quiet and the interior as dark as a pocket.

"Hey! in there," I called.

Presently a sleepy feminine voice answered. "Who's that? What do you want?"

"Bund wants her new slave sent down," I said.

I heard someone moving inside the cave, and almost immediately a woman with dishevelled hair crawled to the entrance. I knew that it was too dark for her to recognize features. All that I could hope for was that she would be too sleepy to have her suspicions aroused by my voice, which I didn't think sounded like the voices of the men I had heard talking. I hoped not, anyway. However, I tried to change it as much as I could, aping Lula's soft tones.

"What does Bund want of her?" she asked.

"How should I know?" I demanded.

"It's very funny," she said. "Bund told me distinctly that I was not to let her out of the cave under any circumstances. Oh, here comes Bund now."

I glanced down. The fight was over, and the women were ascending to their caves. To me that catwalk in front of Bund's cave looked like a most unhealthy place to loiter, and I knew that it would be impossible at this time to do anything for Duare; so I made my exit as gracefully and as quickly as I could.

"I guess Bund changed her mind," I told the woman, as I turned back toward the ladder that led to the upper catwalk. Fortunately for me the slave woman was still half asleep, and doubtless her principal concern at the moment was to get back to her slumbers. She mumbled something about its being very odd, but before she could go deeper into the matter with me I was on my way.

It didn't take me long to clamber the rickety ladder to the catwalk in front of the men's caves and make my way to the last one to the left of the ladder. The interior was as dark as a pocket and smelled as though it needed airing and had needed it for several generations.

"Lula!" I whispered.

I heard a groan. "You again?" asked a querulous voice.

"Your old friend, Carson himself," I replied. "You don't seem glad to see me."

"I'm not. I hoped I'd never see you again. I hoped you'd be killed. Why weren't you killed? You didn't stay there long enough. Why did you come away?"

"I had to come up and see my old friend, Lula," I said.

"And then you will go right away again?"

"Not tonight. Maybe tomorrow. I certainly hope tomorrow."

He groaned again. "Don't let them see you coming out of this cave tomorrow," he begged. "Oh, why did I tell you where my cave was!"

"That was very stupid of you, Lula; but don't worry. I won't get you in any trouble if you help me."

"Help you! Help you get your mate away from Bund? Why, Bund would kill me."

"Well, let's not worry about it until tomorrow. We both need sleep. But say, Lula, don't betray me. If you do, I'll tell Bund the whole story. One more thing. Do you occupy this cave alone?"

"No. Two other men are with me. They'll probably be up soon. Don't talk to me any more after they come."

"You think they'd give us away?"

"I don't know," he admitted; "but I'm not going to take any chances."

After this we relapsed into silence. It wasn't long before we heard footsteps outside, and a moment later the other two men entered the cave. They had been carrying on a conversation, and they brought the tail end of it in with them.

20

"—beat me; so I didn't say any more about it; but just before we came up I heard the women talking about it. Nearly all were in their caves at the time. It was just before we went down to build the fires for the last meal, just before darkness came. I had come out of the cave to go down when I happened to look up and see it."

"Why did your woman beat you?"

"She said I was lying and that she didn't like liars, that she couldn't abide them and that if I'd tell a silly lie like that I'd lie about anything; but now two of the women said they saw it."

"What did your woman say to that?"

"She said I probably had a beating coming to me anyway."

"What did the thing look like?"

"Like a big bird, only it didn't flap its wings. It flew right over the canyon. The women who saw it said it was the same thing they saw sitting on the ground when they captured the new slave today and killed the yellow-haired man."

"That thing must have been the anotar that Lula spoke of."

"But he said he was only joking."

"How could he joke about something he'd never seen? There's something funny about this. Hey, Lula!" There was no response. "Hey, you, Lula!" the man called again.

"I'm asleep," said Lula.

"Then you'd better wake up. We want to know about this anotar," insisted the man.

"I don't know anything about it; I never saw it; I never went up in it."

"Who ever said you went up in it? How could a man go up in the air in anything? It can't be done."

"Oh, yes it can," exclaimed Lula. "Two men can ride in it, maybe four. It flies all around wherever you want it to go."

"I thought you didn't know anything about it."

"I am going asleep," announced Lula.

"You're going to tell us all about that anotar, or I'll tell Bund on you."

"Oh, Vyla! You wouldn't do that?" cried Lula.

"Yes, I would so," insisted Vyla. "You'd better tell us everything."

"If I do, will you promise not to tell *anyone*?"

"I promise."

"And you, Ellie? Will you promise?" asked Lula.

"I wouldn't tell anyone on *you*, Lula; you ought to know *that*," Ellie assured him. "Now, go on and tell us."

"Well, I have seen it; and I've ridden in it—way up in the sky."

"Now you *are* lying, Lula," chided Vyla.

"Honest to gracious, I'm not," insisted Lula, "and if you don't believe *me*, ask Carson."

I had been expecting the nit-wit to spill the beans; so I wasn't greatly surprised. I think that if Lula had had an I.Q. rating it would have been about decimal two.

"And who is Carson?" demanded Vyla.

"He makes the anotar go in the air," explained Lula.

"Well, how can we ask *him*? I think you are lying again, Lula. You are getting into a bad habit of lying, lately."

"I am not lying, and if you don't believe me you can ask Carson. He's right here in this cave."

"What?" demanded the two, in unison.

"Lula is not lying," I said. "I am here; also, Lula rode in the anotar with me. If you two would like to ride, I'll take you up tomorrow—if you can get me out of here without the women seeing me."

For a while there was silence; then Ellie spoke in a rather frightened voice. "What would Jad say if she knew about this?" he asked. Jad was the chief.

"You promised not to tell," Lula reminded him.

"Jad needn't know, unless one of you tells her," I said; "and if you do, I'll say that all three of you knew it and that you were trying to get me to kill her."

"Oh, you wouldn't say that, would you?" cried Ellie.

22

"I certainly would. But if you'll help me, no one need ever know; and you can get a ride in the anotar to boot."

"I'd be afraid," said Ellie.

"It's nothing to be afraid of," said Lula in a voice that swaggered. "I wasn't afraid. You see the whole world all at once, and nothing can get at you. I'd like to stay up there all the time. I wouldn't be afraid of the tharbans then; I wouldn't even be afraid of Bund."

"I'd like to go up," said Vyla. "If Lula wasn't afraid, nobody would be."

"If you go up, I will," promised Ellie.

"I'll go," said Vyla.

Well, we talked a little longer; then, before going to sleep, I asked some questions about the habits of the women, and found that the hunting and raiding parties went out the first thing in the morning and that they left a small guard of warrior women to protect the village. I also learned that the slaves came down in the morning and while the hunting and raiding parties were out, gathered wood for the fires and brought water to the caves in clay jugs. They also helped the men with the making of sandals, loincloths, ornaments, and pottery.

The next morning I stayed in the cave until after the hunters and raiders had left; then I descended the ladders to the ground. I had learned enough about the women to be reasonably certain that I would not arouse their suspicions, as their men are so self-effacing and the women ignore them so completely that a woman might recognize scarcely any of the men other than her mate; but I was not so sure about the men. They all knew one another. What they might do when they recognized a stranger among them was impossible to foresee.

Half a dozen warrior women were loitering in a group near the middle of the canyon while the men and slaves busied themselves with their allotted duties. I saw some of them eyeing me as I reached the ground and walked toward a group down canyon from them where a number of female slaves were working, but they did not accost me.

I kept away from the men as much as possible and approached the female slaves. I was looking for Duare. My heart sank as I saw no sign of her, and I wished that I had gone first to Bund's cave to look for her. Some of the slaves looked at me questioningly; then one of them spoke to me.

"Who are you?" she demanded.

"*You* ought to know," I told her; and while she was puzzling that one out, I walked on.

Presently I saw some slaves emerging from a little side gully with armfuls of wood, and among them I recognized Duare. My heart leaped at sight of her. I sauntered to a point at which she would have to pass me, waiting for the expression in those dear eyes when she should recognize me. Closer and closer she came, and the nearer she got the harder my heart pounded. When she was a couple of steps away, she glanced up into my face; then she passed on without a sign of recognition. For an instant I was crushed; then I was angry, and I turned and overtook her.

"Duare!" I whispered.

She stopped and wheeled toward me. "Carson!" she exclaimed. "Oh, Carson. What has happened to you?"

I had forgotten the black hair and the ugly wounds on my forehead and cheek, the latter an ugly gash from temple to chin. She actually had not known me.

"Oh, but you are not dead; you are not dead! I thought that they had killed you. Tell me—"

"Not now, dear," I said. "We're going to get out of here first."

"But how? What chance have we to escape while they are watching?"

"Simply run away. I don't think we'll ever have a better chance." I glanced quickly about. The warriors were still unconcerned, paying no attention to us or anyone else. They were superior beings who looked with contempt upon men and slaves. Most of the slaves and men were farther up canyon than we, but there were a few that we would have to pass. "Are you going back for more wood?" I asked.

"Yes, we are," she told me.

"Good. When you come back, try to walk at the very rear of the others. I'll follow you into the canyon, if I can; unless a better plan occurs to me. You'd better go on now."

After she left me, I boldly sought out Lula. The men who looked at me eyed me suspiciously, but they are so stupid that they were at first merely puzzled. They didn't think of doing anything about it. I hoped that when they did, it would be too late to interfere with my plans. When I found Lula and he saw who it was, he looked about as happy as he would had he suddenly been confronted by a ghost.

"Get Vyla and Ellie," I told him, "and come with me."

"What for?" he demanded.

"Never mind. Do as I tell you, and do it quickly; or I'll tell those women." He was too dumb to realize immediately that I wouldn't dare do that; so he went and got Ellie and Vyla.

"What do you want of us?" demanded the latter.

"I'm going to take you for that ride in the anotar, just as I promised you last night," I said.

They looked at each other questioningly. I could see that they were afraid—probably frightened by the thought of flying, but more frightened of the women.

Ellie choked. "I can't go today," he said.

"You are coming with me whether you go up in the anotar or not," I told them in no uncertain tones.

"What do you want of us?" asked Vyla.

"Come with me, and I'll show you. And don't forget that if you don't do as I tell you I'll tell the women about that plan of yours to have me kill Jad. Now, come!"

"You're a mean old thing," whined Vyla.

They had been kicked around so much all their lives and had developed such colossal inferiority complexes that they were afraid of everybody; and, if they weren't given too much time to think, would obey anyone's commands; so they came with me.

The wood carriers had laid down their loads and were on their way back to the side gully for more as I herded my unwilling accomplices toward a point the slaves would have to pass; and as they approached, I saw, to my vast relief, that Duare was trailing the others. As she came opposite us, I gathered my three around her to hide her, if possible, from the sight of the warrior women; then I directed them at a loitering gait downward toward the mouth of The Narrow Canyon. Right then I would have given a lot for a rear-sight mirror; for I wanted to see what was going on behind us, but didn't dare look back for fear of suggesting that we were doing something we shouldn't be—it was a case of nonchalance or nothing, and not a cigarette of any brand among us. I never knew minutes to be so long; but finally we approached the lower end of the canyon, and then I heard the hoarse voice of a woman shouting at us.

"Hi, there! Where are you going? Come back here!"

With that, the three men stopped in their tracks; and I knew that the jig was up as far as secrecy was concerned. I look Duare's hand, and we kept on down the canyon. Now I could look back. Lula, Vyla and Ellie were marching back to their masters; and three of the women were coming down the canyon toward us. When they saw that two of us had ignored their command and were walking on, they commenced to shout again; and when we didn't pay any attention to them they broke into a trot; then we took to our heels. I didn't doubt but that we could outdistance them, for they were not built for speed. However, we would have to get to the ship far enough ahead of them to give us time to untie her before they overtook us.

As we turned out of the mouth of The Narrow Canyon into the wide canyon of which it is a branch, we came on fairly level ground sloping gently in the direction we were going. Groups of splendid trees dotted the landscape, and off there somewhere in the near beyond was the ship and safety; then, squarely across our path and a couple of hundred yards away, I saw three tharbans.

IV: A NEW LAND

The sight of those three great beasts barring our way was just about as discouraging as anything I have ever encountered. Of course I had my pistol; but the rays don't always kill immediately any more than bullets do, and even if I should succeed in killing them the delay would permit the women to overtake us. I could hear them shouting, and I was afraid their voices might reach one of the hunting parties; so, all in all, I was in a tough spot. Fortunately, they hadn't come out of The Narrow Canyon yet; and I thought I saw a possible chance of eluding them and the tharbans. We were close to a group of trees the dense foliage of which would form an excellent hiding place; so I hoisted Duare to a lower branch and swung up after her. Climbing well up, we waited. Through the foliage we could look out, though I doubted that anyone could see us.

The three tharbans had witnessed our ruse and were coming toward the tree, but when the running warrior women hove into sight out of the mouth of The Narrow Canyon the beasts paid no more attention to us, but turned their attention to the women instead. The sight of the tharbans brought the women to a sudden stop. I saw them looking around for us; and then, as the tharbans advanced, they retreated into The Narrow Canyon. The three beasts followed them, and the moment that all were out of sight Duare and I dropped to the ground and continued on toward the ship.

We could hear the roars and growls of the tharbans and the shouts of the women growing fainter in the distance as we almost ran in our eagerness to reach the anotar. What had appeared a few moments before almost a catastrophe had really proved our salvation, for now we had no need to fear pursuit from the village. My only immediate concern now was the ship, and I can tell you that I breathed a sigh of relief when we came in sight of it and I saw that it was intact. Five minutes later we were in the air, and the adventure of Houtomai was a thing of the past. Yet, how near it had come to meaning death for me and a life of slavery for Duare! If the warrior women had taken but an extra moment to make sure that I was dead how very different the outcome would have been. I shall always think that fear of the ship, a thing so strange to them, caused them to hurry away. Duare says that they talked much about the ship on the way back to the village and that it was evident that they were troubled by it, not being quite sure that it was not some strange beast that might pursue them.

We had much to talk about as I circled in search of game, that I might make another kill; for I had not eaten for two days, and Duare only a few mean scraps while she was the slave of Bund. Duare kept looking at me and touching me to make sure that I was alive, so certain had she been that the Samaryans had killed me.

"I should not have lived long, Carson, if you hadn't come," she said. "With you dead, I didn't care to live—certainly not in slavery. I was only waiting for an opportunity to destroy myself."

I located a herd of antelope-like animals and made my kill much as I had the previous day, but this time Duare kept vigilant lookout while I attended to the butchering; then we flew to the island where Lula and I had stopped while I transformed myself into a brunette. This time I reversed the operation, after we had cooked and eaten some of our meat. Once again we were happy and contented. Our recent troubles now seemed very remote, so quickly does the spirit of man rebound from depression and push black despair into the limbo of forgetfulness.

Duare was much concerned about my wounds and insisted on bathing them herself. The only danger, of course, was from infection; and we had no means of disinfecting them. Naturally there was much less danger than there would have been on Earth, where overpopulation and increased means of transportation have greatly spread and increased the numbers of malignant bacteria. Also, the longevity serum with which I had been inoculated by Danus shortly after my arrival upon Amtor gave me considerable immunity. All in all, I was not much concerned; but Duare was like a hen with one chicken. She had finally given in to her natural inclinations; and, having admitted her love, she was lavishing on its object the devotion and solicitude which raise love to its purest and most divine heights.

We were both of us pretty well done in by all that we had been through, and so we decided to remain at the island until the following day at least. I was quite sure that there were no men and no dangerous beasts there, and for the first time in many months we could utterly relax without concern about the safety of our self or that of the other. Those were the most perfect twenty-four hours I had ever spent.

The next day we took off from our little island with real regret and flew south along the valley of The River of Death down toward the ocean into which we knew it must empty. But what ocean? What lay beyond it? Where in all this vast world could we go?

"Perhaps we can find another little island somewhere," Duare suggested, "and live there always, just you and I alone."

I didn't have the heart to tell her that in a few months we'd probably be wanting to knife one another. I was really in a quandary. It was impossible that we return to Vepaja. I knew now definitely that Duare would rather die than be separated from me; and there was no question but that I should be executed the moment Mintep, her father, got his hands on me. My only reason for planning to take Duare back to Vepaja had been my sincere belief that, no matter what became of me, she would be happier there eventually and certainly much safer than roaming around this savage world with a man absolutely without a country; but now I knew differently. I knew that either of us would rather be dead than permanently separated from the other.

"We'll make a go of it some way," I told her, "and if there's a spot on Amtor where we can find peace and safety we'll locate it."

"We have fifty years before the anotar falls to pieces," said Duare, with a laugh.

We had flown but a short time before I saw what appeared to be a large body of water dead ahead, and such it soon proved to be. We had come to the ocean at last.

"Let's go out over it and look for our island," said Duare.

"We'd better stock up with food and water first," I suggested.

I had wrapped the remainder of our meat in the large, waxy leaves I had found growing on the little island; and was sure that it would keep for several days, but of course we didn't want to eat it raw; and as we couldn't cook it while flying, there was nothing to do but land and cook the meat. I also wanted to gather some fruits and nuts and a tuber that grows almost everywhere on Amtor and is quite palatable and nutritious—palatable even when eaten raw.

I found an open flat that extended back from The River of Death for several miles. It was forest bordered on one side, and a little river ran through it down to the larger stream from mountains to the east. I made a landing near the forest in the hope that I would find such fruits and nuts as I desired, nor was I disappointed. After gathering them, I loaded some firewood into the rear cockpit and taxied over beside the small stream. Here we were in the open where we could see the surrounding country in all directions and therefore in no danger of being surprised by either man or beast. I built a fire and cooked our meat while Duare kept watch. I also filled the water tank with which I had equipped the ship at the time it was built. We now had food and water sufficient for several days, and filled with the spirit of exploration we took off and headed out to sea, passing over the great delta of The River of Death, a river that must rival the Amazon.

From the first, Duare had been keenly interested in the navigation of the ship. I had explained the purpose and operation of the controls, but she had not actually flown the anotar herself. Now I let her try it, for I knew that she must learn to fly against the possibility of our being in the air for long periods such as might be necessitated by a transoceanic flight. I would have to have sleep, and this would not be possible in the air unless Duare could fly the ship. Now, flying a ship in the air under ordinary weather conditions is not even so difficult as walking; so it required only a few minutes to establish her confidence and give her something of the feel of the ship. I knew that practice would give her smoothness, and I had her fly at an altitude that would permit me to come to the rescue if she got in any trouble.

We flew all that night with Duare at the controls about a third of the time, and when morning broke I sighted land. As far as I could see to the east and west the boles and foliage of great trees rose thousands of feet to disappear in the inner cloud envelope which floats forever over the entire expanse of Amtor, a second defense to the outer cloud envelope against the intense heat of the sun that would otherwise burn the surface of the planet to a crisp.

"That aspect looks familiar," I said to Duare when she awoke.

"What do you mean?" she asked.

"I think it is Vepaja. We'll skirt the coast, and if I'm right we will see the natural harbor where the Sofal and the Sovong lay at anchor the day that you were kidnaped and Kamlot and I were captured by the klangan. I'm sure I shall recognize it."

Duare said nothing. She was silent for a long time as we flew along the coast. Presently I saw the harbor.

"There it is," I said. "This is Vepaja, Duare."

"Vepaja," she breathed.

"We are here, Duare. Do you want to stay?"

She shook her head. "Not without you." I leaned toward her and kissed her.

"Where then?" I asked.

"Oh, let's just keep on going. One direction's as good as another."

The ship, at the time, was flying perhaps a couple of points north of west; so I simply maintained that course. The world ahead of us was absolutely unknown, as far as we were concerned; and as this course would keep us away from the antarctic regions and well into the northern part of the south temperate zone, it seemed as good a course to hold as any. In the opposite direction lay the stronghold of the Thorists, where we could hope to find only captivity and death.

As the long day wore away, nothing but illimitable ocean stretched monotonously before us. The ship functioned beautifully. It could not function otherwise, since into its construction had gone the best that the finest scientific minds of Havatoo could give. The design had been mine, as aircraft were absolutely undreamed of in Havatoo prior to my coming; but the materials, the motor, the fuel were exclusively Amtorian. For strength, durability, and lightness the first would be impossible of duplication on Earth; the motor was a marvel of ingenuity, compactness, power and durability combined with lightness of weight; the fuel I have already described. In design the ship was more or less of a composite of those with which I was familiar or had myself flown on Earth. It seated four, two abreast in an open front cockpit and two in a streamlined cabin aft; there were controls in both cockpits, and the ship could be flown from any of the four seats. As I have before stated, it was an amphibian.

During the long day I varied the monotony by instructing Duare in landings and take-offs, there being a gentle westerly breeze. We had to keep a sharp lookout at these times for the larger denizens of the sea, some of which might easily have wrecked the ship had their dispositions been as fearsome as their appearance.

As night fell, the vast Amtorian scene was bathed in the soft, mysterious, nocturnal light that beneficient Nature has vouchsafed a moonless planet. Seemingly as limitless as interstellar space, the endless sea rolled to the outer rim of our universe, glowing wanly. No land, no ship, no living thing impinged, upon the awful serenity of the scene—only our silent plane and we two infinitesimal atoms wandering aimlessly through space. Duare moved a little closer to me. Companionship was good in this infinite loneliness.

During the night the wind veered and blew from the south, and at dawn I saw cloud banks rolling in ahead of us. The air was much cooler. It was evident that we were getting the tail end of a south polar storm. I didn't like the looks of that fog. I had blind flying instruments on the instrument board; but, even so, who would care to fly blind in a world concerning the topography of which he knew nothing? Nor was I particularly keen to chance waiting the fog out on the surface of the sea. The chances are it would have been safe enough, but I had seen far too many leviathans cavorting about in the waters beneath us to incline me toward spending any more time on the surface of the water than was absolutely necessary. I determined to change our course and fly north ahead of the fog. It was then that Duare pointed ahead.

"Isn't that land?" she asked.

"It certainly has all the appearances of land," I said, after taking a long look.

"Maybe it is our island," she suggested laughingly.

"We'll go and have a look at it before the fog rolls over it. We can always beat that fog if it gets too thick."

"Land will look pretty good again," said Duare.

"Yes," I agreed. "We've been looking at an awful lot of water."

As we approached the coast line we saw mountains in the distance and far to the northwest what appeared to be one of those giant tree forests such as cover almost the entire area of the island of Vepaja.

"Oh, there's a city!" exclaimed Duare.

"So it is—a seaport. Quite a good-sized city, too. I wonder what kind of people live there."

Duare shook her head. "I don't know. There is a land northwest of Vepaja that is called Anlap. I have seen it on the map. It lies partially in Trabol and partially in Strabol. The maps show it as an island, a very large island; but of course nobody knows. Strabol has never been thoroughly explored."

It seemed to me that none of Venus had ever been thoroughly explored, nor could I wonder. The most able men I had met here clung to the belief that it was a saucer-shaped world floating on a molten sea. They thought that its greatest circumference lay at what I knew to be the south pole, and on their maps the equator was not even a dot. They never dreamed of the existence of another hemisphere. With maps based on such erroneous reasoning, everything was distorted; and because their maps were therefore useless, no navigator dared go far from familiar waters and seldom out of sight of land.

As we approached the city I saw that it was walled and heavily fortified, and closer inspection revealed the fact that it was being beleaguered by a large force. The hum of Amtorian guns came faintly to our ears. We saw the defenders on the walls; and, beyond the walls, we saw the enemy—long lines of men encircling the city, each lying behind his shield. These shields are composed of metal more or less impervious to both r-rays and T-rays; and their use must result in far more mobile attacking forces than could have been possible were the men facing earthly bullets; it practically amounted to each man carrying his own trench. The troops could be maneuvered almost anywhere on the field of battle while under fire, with a minimum of casualties.

As we passed over the city, firing practically ceased on both sides. We could see thousands of faces upturned toward us, and I could imagine the wonder and amazement that the ship must have engendered in the minds of those thousands of soldiers and civilians, not one of whom could possibly have conceived the nature of this giant, birdlike thing speeding silently above them. As every portion of the ship, whether wood, metal, or fabric, had been sprayed with a solution of this ray-resisting substance I felt quite safe in flying low above the contending forces; and so I spiralled downward and, circling, flew close above the city's wall. Then I leaned out and waved my hand. A great shout rose from the men within the city, but the attackers were silent for a moment; then a volley of shots were directed at us.

The ship might have been coated with ray-resisting material; but Duare and I were not, and so I zoomed to a safer altitude and turned the ship's nose inland to reconnoiter farther. Beyond the lines of the investing forces we flew over their main camp, beyond which a broad highway led toward the southwest, from which direction troops were marching toward the camp; and there were long trains of wagons drawn by huge, elephantine animals, and men mounted on strange beasts, and big T-ray guns, and all the other impedimenta of a great army on the march.

Turning toward the north, I reconnoitered in search of information. I wanted to know something about this country and the disposition of its inhabitants. From what I had already seen, their dispositions seemed unequivocally warlike; but somewhere there might be a peaceful, hospitable city where strangers would be treated with consideration. What I was looking for was a single individual whom I might question without risking injury to Duare or myself, for to have made a landing among those fighting men would probably have been fatal—especially among comrades of the contingent that had fired on us. The attitude of the defenders of the city had been more friendly; but still I couldn't risk a landing there without knowing something about them, nor did it seem the part of wisdom to land in a beleaguered city that, from the number of its attackers, might be taken any day. Duare and I were looking for peace, not war.

I covered a considerable area of territory without seeing a human being, but at last I discovered a lone man coming out of a canyon in the hills several miles north of the big camp I have mentioned. As I dropped toward him, he turned and looked up. He did not run; but stood his ground, and I saw him draw the pistol at his hip.

"Don't fire!" I called to him as I glided past. "We are friends."

"What do you want?" he shouted back.

I circled and flew back, landing a couple of hundred yards from him. "I am a stranger here," I shouted to him. "I want to ask for information."

He approached the ship quite boldly, but he kept his weapon in readiness for any eventuality. I dropped down from the cockpit and went forward to meet him, raising my right hand to show that it held no weapon. He raised his left—he wasn't taking any chances; but the gesture signified a friendly attitude, or at least not a belligerent one.

A half smile touched his lips as I descended from the ship. "So you *are* a human being, after all," he said. "At first I didn't know but that you were a part of that thing, whatever it is. Where are you from? What do you want of me?"

"We are strangers here," I told him. "We do not even know in what country we are. We want to know the disposition of the people here toward strangers, and if there is a city where we might be received hospitably."

"This is the land of Anlap," he said, "and we are in the Kingdom of Korva."

"What city is that back by the sea? There was fighting going on there."

"You saw fighting?" he demanded. "How was it going? Had the city fallen?" He seemed eager for news.

"The city had not fallen," I said, "and the defenders seemed in good spirits."

He breathed a sigh of relief. Suddenly his brow clouded. "How do I know you're not a Zani spy?" he demanded.

I shrugged. "You don't," I said, "but I'm not. I don't even know what a Zani is."

"No, you couldn't be," he said presently. "With that yellow hair of yours I don't know what you could be—certainly not of our race."

"Well, how about answering some of my questions?" I inquired with a smile.

He smiled in return. "That's right. You wanted to know the disposition of the people of Korva to strangers and the name of the city by the sea. Well, before the Zanis seized the government, you would have been treated well in any Korvan city. But now it is different. Sanara, the city you asked about, would welcome you; it has not yet fallen under the domination of the Zanis. They are trying to reduce it now, and if it capitulates the last stronghold of freedom in Korva will have fallen."

"You are from Sanara?" I asked.

"Yes, at present. I had always lived in Amlot, the capitol, until the Zanis came into power; then I couldn't go back, because I had been fighting them."

"I just flew over a big camp south of here," I said; "was that a Zani camp?"

"Yes. I'd give anything to see it. How many men have they?"

"I don't know; but it's a large camp, and more soldiers and supplies are coming in from the southwest."

"From Amlot," he said. "Oh, if I could but see that!"

"You can," I told him.

"How?" he demanded.

I pointed toward the ship. He looked just a little bit taken aback, but only for a second.

"All right," he said. "You will not regret your kindness. May I ask your name? Mine is Taman."

"And mine is Carson."

He looked at me curiously. "What country are you from? I have never before seen an Amtorian with yellow hair."

"It is a long story," I said. "Suffice it to say that I am not an Amtorian; I am from another world."

We walked toward the ship together, he, in the meantime, having returned his pistol to its holster. When we reached it, he saw Duare for the first time. I could just note a faint expression of surprise, which he hid admirably. He was evidently a man of refinement. I introduced them, and then showed him how to enter the rear cockpit and fasten his lifebelt.

Of course I couldn't see him when we took off, but he afterward told me that he believed his end had come. I flew him directly back to the Zani camp and along the highway toward Amlot.

"This is wonderful!" he exclaimed time and again. "I can see everything. I can even count the battalions and the guns and the wagons."

"Tell me when you've seen enough," I said.

"I think I've seen all that's necessary. Poor Sanara! How can it withstand such a horde? And I may not even be able to get back and make my report. The city must be surrounded by troops by now. I just barely got out an *ax* ago." An *ax* is equivalent to twenty days of Amtorian time, or slightly over twenty-two days, eleven hours of Earth time.

"The city is entirely surrounded," I told him. "I doubt that you could possibly pass through the lines even at night."

"Would you—" he hesitated.

"Would I what?" I asked, though I guessed what he wished to ask me.

"But no," he said; "it would be too much to ask of a stranger. You would be risking your life and that of your companion."

"Is there any place large enough for me to land inside the walls of Sanara?" I asked.

He laughed. "You guessed well," he said. "How much space do you require?"

I told him.

"Yes," he said; "there is a large field near the center of town where races were held. You could land there easily."

"A couple of more questions," I suggested.

"Certainly! Ask as many as you please."

"Have you sufficient influence with the military authorities to insure our safety? I am, of course, thinking of my mate. I cannot risk harm befalling her."

"I give you the word of a nobleman that you will both be safe under my protection," he assured me.

"And that we shall be permitted to leave the city whenever we choose, and that our ship will not be molested or detained?"

"Again you have my word for all that you have asked," he said; "but still I think it is too much to ask of you—too much to permit you to do for a stranger."

I turned to Duare. "What is your answer, Duare?" I asked.

"I think that I shall like Sanara," she said.

I turned the ship's nose in the direction of the Korvan seaport.

V: SANARA

Taman was profuse in his gratitude, but not too profuse. I felt from the first that he was going to prove a likable fellow; and I know that Duare liked him, too. She ordinarily seldom enters into conversation with strangers. The old taboos of the jong's daughter are not to be easily dispelled, but she talked with Taman on the flight to Sanara, asking him many questions.

"You will like our people," he told her. "Of course, now, under the strain of a long siege, conditions are not normal nor are the people; but they will welcome you and treat you well. I shall take you both into my own home, where I know that my wife can make you comfortable even under the present conditions."

As we passed over the Zanis' lines they commenced to take pot shots at us, but I was flying too high for their fire to have been effective even against an unprotected ship. Taman and I had discussed the matter of landing. I was a little fearful that the defenders might become frightened at this strange craft were it to attempt a landing in the city, especially as this time we would be approaching from enemy country. I suggested a plan which he thought might work out satisfactorily; so he wrote a note on a piece of paper which he had and tied it to one of the large nuts we had brought with us. In fact he wrote several notes, tying each one to a different nut. Each note stated that he was in the anator they saw flying above the city and asked the commander to have the racing field cleared so that we could make a safe landing. If the note were received and permission to land was granted, they were to send several men with flags to the windward end of the field with instructions to wave them until they saw us come in for a landing. This would accomplish two purposes—show us that we would not be fired on and also give me the direction of the wind at the field.

I dropped the notes at intervals over the city, and then circled at a safe distance awaiting the outcome of our plan. I could see the field quite distinctly, and that there were quite a few people on it—far too many to make a landing safe. Anyway, there was nothing to do but wait for the signal. While we were waiting, Taman pointed out places of interest in the city—parks, public buildings, barracks, the governor's palace. He said that the jong's nephew lived there now and ruled as jong, his uncle being a prisoner of the Zanis at Amlot. There were even rumors that the jong had been executed. It was that that the defenders of Sanara feared as much as they feared the Zanis, because they didn't trust the jong's nephew and didn't want him as permanent jong.

It seemed as though we'd circled over the city for an hour before we received any indication that our notes had been received; then I saw soldiers clearing the people out of the racing field. That was a good omen; then a dozen soldiers with flags went to one end of the field and commenced to wave them. At that I commenced to drop in a tight spiral—you see I didn't want to go too near the city walls for fear of attracting the fire of the Zanis.

Looking down, I saw people converging upon that field from all directions. The word that we were going to land must have spread like wildfire. They were coming in droves, blocking the avenues. I hoped that a sufficient detail of soldiers had been sent to keep them from swarming over the field and tearing us and the plane to pieces. I was so worried that I zoomed upward again and told Taman to write another note asking for a large military guard to keep the people away from the ship. This he did, and then I dropped down again and tossed the note out on the field near a group of men that Taman told me were officers. Five minutes later we saw a whole battalion marched onto the field and posted around the edges; then I came in for a landing.

Say, but weren't those people thrilled! They were absolutely breathless and silent until the ship rolled almost to a stop; then they burst into loud cheering. It certainly made me feel pretty good to realize that we were welcome somewhere in the world, for our situation had previously seemed utterly hopeless, realizing, as we did from past experience, that strangers are seldom welcome in any Amtorian city. My own experience on the occasion of my landing in Vepaja from my rocket ship had borne this out; for, though I was finally accepted, I had been a virtual prisoner in the palace of the jong for a long period of time.

After Taman alighted from the ship, I started to help Duare out; and as she stepped onto the wing in full view of the crowd the cheering stopped and there was a moment of breathless silence; then they burst forth again. It was a wonderful ovation they gave Duare. I think they hadn't realized that the third member of the party was a woman until she stepped into full view. The realization that it was a woman, coupled with her startling beauty, just simply took their breath away. You may be sure that I loved the people of Sanara from that moment.

Several officers had approached the ship, and there were greetings and introductions of course. I noted the deference they accorded Taman, and I realized my good fortune in having placed a really important man under obligations to me. Just how important a personage he really was, I was not to learn until later.

While we had been circling the field I had noticed a number of the huge animals, such as I had seen drawing the gun carriages and army wagons of the Zanis, standing at one side of the field behind the crowd. Several of the beasts were now brought onto the field and up to the ship, or as close as their drivers could urge them; for they were quite evidently afraid of this strange thing. I now got my first close view of a gantor. The animal was larger than an African elephant and had legs very similar to those of that animal, but here the likeness ceased. The head was bull-like and armed with a stout horn about a foot long that grew out of the center of the forehead; the mouth was large, and the powerful jaws

38

were armed with very large teeth; the coat, back of the shoulders, was short and a light tawny yellow marked with white splotches like a pinto horse; while covering the shoulders and short neck was a heavy dark mane; the tail was like that of a bull; three enormous horny toes covered the entire bottoms of the feet, forming hoofs. The driver of each animal sat on the mane above the shoulders; and behind him, on the creature's long, broad back was an open howdah capable of seating a dozen people. That, at least, describes the howdah of the first beast I noted closely. I saw later that there are many forms of howdahs, and in fact the one on the animal that was brought to carry Duare, Taman, and me from the field was a very ornate howdah seating four. Along the left side of each gantor a ladder was lashed, and when the drivers had coaxed their mounts as close as they could to the ship each driver dropped to the ground and set his ladder up against his beast's side. Up these ladders the passengers climbed to the howdahs. I watched the whole procedure with interest, wondering how the driver was going to regain his seat if he lashed the ladder back to the gantor's side or what he would do with the ladder if he used it to climb back onto the gantor.

Well, I soon had my curiosity satisfied. Each driver lashed his ladder back in place against the gantor's side; then he walked around in front of the gantor and gave a command. Instantly the animal lowered its head until its nose almost touched the ground, which brought its horn into a horizontal position about three feet above the ground. The driver climbed onto the horn and gave another command, the gantor raised its head, and the driver stepped to its poll and from there to his seat above the shoulders.

The howdahs of the other gantors were filled with officers and soldiers who acted as our escort from the field, some preceding and some following us off the field and along a broad avenue. As we passed, the people raised their hands in salute, the arms extended at an angle of about forty-five degrees, their palms crossed. I noticed that they did this only as our gantor approached; and I soon realized that they were saluting Taman, as he acknowledged the salutes by bowing to the right and left. So once again I had evidence that he was a man of importance.

The people on the street wore the scant apparel that is common on Amtor, where it is usually warm and sultry; and they also wore, according to what seems to be a universal custom, daggers and swords, the women the former, the men both. The soldiers among them also carried pistols slung in holsters at their hips. They were a very nice, clean looking people with pleasant faces. The buildings facing the avenue were stuccoed; but of what materials they were built, I did not know. The architectural lines were simple but most effective; and notwithstanding the simpleness of the designs, the builders had achieved a diversity that gave pleasing contrasts.

As we proceeded and turned into another avenue the buildings became larger and more beautiful, but still the same simplicity of line was apparent. As we were approaching a rather large building, Taman told me it was the palace of the governor, where the nephew of the jong lived and ruled in the absence of his uncle. We stopped in front of another large home directly across the street from the governor's palace. A guard of soldiers stood before an enormous gate built in the center of the front wall, which was flush with the sidewalk. They saluted Taman, and swung the gate open. Our escort had previously moved back across the avenue, and now our driver guided his huge mount through the gateway along a wide corridor into an enormous courtyard where there were trees and flowers and fountains. This was the palace of Taman.

A small army of people poured from the building, whom, of course, I could not identify but whom I learned later were officers and officials of the palace, retainers, and slaves. They greeted Taman with the utmost deference, but their manner indicated real affection.

"Inform the janjong that I have returned and am bringing guests to her apartments," Taman directed one of the officers.

Now janjong means, literally, daughter of a jong; in other words, a princess. It is the official title of the daughter of a living jong, but it is often used through life as a courtesy title after a jong dies. A tanjong, son of a jong, is a prince.

Taman himself showed us our apartments, knowing that we would wish to freshen ourselves up before being presented to the janjong. Women slaves took Duare in hand and a man slave showed me my bath and brought me fresh apparel.

Our apartments, consisting of three rooms and two baths, were beautifully decorated and furnished. It must have been like heaven to Duare who had known nothing of either beauty or comfort since she had been stolen from her father's palace over a year before.

When we were ready an officer came and conducted us to a small reception room on the same floor but at the opposite end of the palace. Here Taman was awaiting us. He asked me how we should be introduced to the janjong, and when I told him Duare's title I could see that he was both pleased and surprised. As for myself, I asked him to introduce me as Carson of Venus. Of course the word Venus meant nothing to him, as the planet is known to the inhabitants as Amtor. We were then ushered into the presence of the janjong. The formality of introductions on Amtor are both simple and direct; there is no circumlocution. We were led into the presence of a most beautiful woman, who arose and smiled as we approached her.

"This is my wife, Jahara, janjong of Korva," announced Taman; then he turned to Duare. "This is Duare, janjong of Vepaja, wife of Carson of Venus," and, indicating me, "This is Carson of Venus." It was all very simple. Of course Taman didn't say wife—there is no marriage among any of the peoples I have known on Amtor. A couple merely agree between themselves to live together, and they are ordinarily as faithful to one another as married couples on Earth are supposed to be. They may separate and take other mates if they choose, but they rarely do. Since the serum of longevity was discovered many

40

couples have lived together for a thousand years in perfect harmony—possibly because the tie that bound them was not a fetter. The word that Taman used instead of wife was ooljaganja—lovewoman. I like it.

During our visit with Taman and Jahara we learned many things concerning them and Korva. Following a disastrous war, in which the resources of the nation had been depleted, a strange cult had arisen conceived and led by a common soldier named Mephis. He had usurped all the powers of government, seized Amlot, the capital, and reduced the principal cities of Korva with the exception of Sanara, to which many of the nobility had flocked with their loyal retainers. Mephis had imprisoned Jahara's father, Kord, hereditary jong of Korva, because he would not accede to the demand of the Zanis and rule as a figurehead dominated by Mephis. Recently rumors had reached Sanara that Kord had been assassinated, that Mephis would offer the jongship to some member of the royal family, that he would assume the title himself; but no one really knew anything about it.

We also inferred, though no direct statement to that effect was made, that the jong's nephew, Muso, acting jong, was none too popular. What we didn't learn until much later was that Taman, who was of royal blood, was directly in line for the throne after Muso and that Muso was intensely jealous of Taman's popularity with all classes of people. When we had picked Taman up behind the enemy lines he had been returning from a most hazardous assignment upon which Muso had sent him, possibly in the hope that he would never return.

Food was served in the apartments of Jahara; and while we were eating, an officer of the jong was announced. He brought a gracefully worded intimation that Muso would be glad to receive us immediately if Taman and Jahara would bring us to the palace and present us. It was, of course, a command.

We found Muso and his consort, Illana, in the audience room of the palace surrounded by a considerable retinue. They were seated on impressive thrones, and it was evident that Muso was taking his jongship very seriously. So great was his dignity that he did not condescend to smile, though he was courteous enough. The closest his equilibrium came to being upset was when his eyes fell on Duare. I could see that her beauty impressed him, but I was accustomed to that—it usually startled people.

He kept us in the audience chamber only long enough to conclude the formalities; then he led us into a smaller room.

"I saw the strange thing in which you fly as it circled above the city," he said. "What do you call it? and what keeps it in the air?"

I told him that Duare had christened it an anotar, and then I explained briefly the principle of heavier-than-air craft flight.

"Has it any practical value?" he asked.

"In the world from which I come airlines have been established that transport passengers, mail, and express between all the large cities and to every portion of the world; civilized governments maintain great fleets of planes for military purposes."

"But how could an anotar be used for military purposes?" he asked.

"For reconnaissance, for one thing," I told him. "I flew Taman over the enemy camp and along its line of communication. They can be used for destroying supply bases, for disabling batteries, even for direct attack upon enemy troops."

"How could your ship be used against the Zanis?" he asked.

"By bombing their lines, their camp, and their supply depots and trains we might lower their morale. Of course with but a single ship we could not accomplish much."

"I am not so sure of that," said Taman. "The psychological effect of this new engine of destruction might be far more effective than you imagine."

"I agree with Taman," said Muso.

"I shall be glad to serve the jong of Korva in any way," I said.

"Will you accept a commission under me?" he asked. "It will mean that you must swear allegiance to the jong of Korva."

"Why not?" I asked. "I have no country on Amtor, and the ruler and people of Sanara have accorded us courtesy and hospitality," and so I took the oath of allegiance to Korva and was commissioned a captain in the army of the jong. Now, at last, I had a country; but I also had a boss. That part of it I didn't like so well, for, if I am nothing else, I am a rugged individualist.

VI: A SPY

The next few weeks were filled with interest and excitement. The Sanarans manufactured both r-ray and T-ray bombs as well as incendiary bombs, and I made almost daily flights over the enemy lines and camp. In the latter and along their line of communication I wrought the most havoc, but a single ship could not win a war. On several occasions I so demoralized their front line that successful sorties were made by the Sanarans during which prisoners were taken. From these we learned the repeated bombings had had their effect on the morale of the enemy and that an enormous reward had been offered by the Zani chief, Mephis, for the destruction of the ship or for my capture dead or alive.

During these weeks we remained the guests of Taman and Jahara, and were entertained frequently by Muso, the acting jong, and his wife, Illana. The latter was a quiet, self-effacing woman of high lineage but of no great beauty. Muso usually ignored her; and when he didn't, his manner toward her was often brusque and almost offensive; but she was uniformly sweet and unresentful. He was far more attentive to Duare than he was to his own wife, but that is oftentimes a natural reaction of a host in his endeavor to please a guest. While we did not admire it, we could understand it.

The siege of Sanara was almost a stalemate. The city had enormous reserve supplies of synthetic foods; and its water supply was assured by artesian wells, nor was there any dearth of ammunition. The besiegers could not get into the city, and the besieged could not get out. So matters stood one day a month after my arrival in Sanara when Muso sent for me. He was pacing back and forth the width of a small audience chamber when I was ushered into his presence. He appeared nervous and ill at ease. I supposed at the time that he was worried over the seeming hopelessness of raising the siege, for it was of that he spoke first. Later he came to the point.

"I have a commission for you, Captain," he said. "I want to get a message through to one of my secret agents in Amlot. With your ship you can easily cross the enemy lines and reach the vicinity of Amlot without the slightest danger of being captured. I can direct you to a spot where you can make contact with persons who can get you into the city. After that it will be up to you. This must be a secret expedition on your part—no one but you and I must know of it, not even Taman, not even your wife. You will leave the first thing in the morning ostensibly on a bombing expedition, and you will not come back—at least not until you have fulfilled your mission. After that there will be no need for secrecy. If you succeed, I shall create you a noble—specifically an ongvoo—and when the war is over and peace restored I shall see that you receive lands and a palace."

Now, the title ongvoo means, literally, exalted one and is hereditary in the collateral branches of the royal family, though occasionally conferred on members of the nobility for highly meritorious service to the jong. It seemed to me at the time that the service I was commissioned to perform did not merit any such reward, but I gave the matter little thought. It would have been better had I done so.

Muso stepped to a desk and took two thin leather containers, like envelopes, from a drawer. "These contain the messages you are to deliver," he said. "Taman tells me that as you are from another world you probably do not read Amtorian; so you will write in your own language on the outside of each the names and location of those to whom you are to deliver these." He handed me a pen and one of the containers. "This one you will deliver to Lodas at his farm five klookob northwest of Amlot. I shall give you a map with the location marked on it. Lodas will see that you get into Amlot. There you will deliver this other message to a man named Spehon from whom you will receive further instructions."

From another drawer in the desk he took a map and spread it on the table. "Here," he said, making a mark on the map a little northwest of Amlot, "is a flat-topped hill that you will easily be able to locate from the air. It rises between two streams that join one another just southeast of it. In the fork of these two streams lies the farm of Lodas. You will not divulge to Lodas the purpose of your mission or the name of the man you are to meet in Amlot."

"But how am I to find Spehon?" I asked.

"I am coming to that. He is posing as a Zani, and stands high in the councils of Mephis. His office is in the palace formerly occupied by my uncle, Kord, the jong of Korva. You will have no difficulty in locating him. Now, of course you can't be safe in Amlot with that yellow hair of yours. It would arouse immediate suspicion. With black hair you will be safe enough if you do not talk too much, for, while they will know that you are not a member of the Zani party, that will arouse no suspicion as not all of the citizens of Amlot are members of the party, even though they may be loyal to Mephis."

"How will they know that I'm not a member of the party?" I asked.

"Zanis distinguish themselves by a peculiar form of haircut," he explained. "They shave their heads except for a ridge of hair about two inches wide that runs from the forehead to the nape of the neck. I think you understand your instructions, do you not?"

I told him that I did.

"Then here are the envelopes and the map; and here, also, is a bottle of dye to color your hair after you leave Sanara."

"You have thought of everything," I said.

"I usually do," he remarked with a smile. "Now is there anything you'd like to ask before you leave?"

"Yes," I said. "I should like to ask your permission to tell my wife that I shall be away for some time. I do not wish to cause her unnecessary worry."

He shook his head. "That is impossible," he said. "No one must know. There are spies everywhere. If I find that she is unduly alarmed, I promise you that I shall reassure her. You will leave early tomorrow morning. I wish you luck."

That seemed to close the audience; so I saluted and turned to leave. Before I reached the door he spoke again. "You are sure you cannot read Amtorian?" he asked.

I thought the question a little strange and his tone a little too eager. Perhaps it was this, I don't know what else it could have been, that impelled me to reply as I did.

"If that is necessary," I said, "perhaps you had better send some one else. I could fly him to Lodas's farm and bring him back when his mission is completed."

"Oh, no," he hastened to assure me. "It will not be necessary for you to read Amtorian." Then he dismissed me. Of course, having studied under Danus in the palace of the jong of Vepaja, I could read Amtorian quite as well as Muso himself.

All that evening I felt like a traitor to Duare; but I had sworn allegiance to Muso, and while I served him I must obey his orders. The next morning, as I kissed her goodby, I suddenly had a premonition that it might be for the last time. I held her close, dreading to leave her; and she must have sensed in the tenseness of my body that something was amiss.

She looked up at me questioningly. "There is something wrong, Carson," she said. "What is it?"

"It is just that this morning I hate to leave you even more than usual." Then I kissed her and left.

Following a plan of my own to deceive the enemy as to my possible destination, I flew east out over the ocean, turning north when I had passed beyond the range of their vision; then I circled to the west far north of their camp and finally came to the ocean again west of Amlot. Flying back parallel with the coast and a few miles inland I had no difficulty in locating the flat-topped hill that was my principal landmark. During the flight I had dyed my hair black and removed the insignia of my office and service from the scant trappings that, with my loincloth, constituted my apparel. Now I could pass as an ordinary citizen of Amlot, providing no one noticed the color of my eyes.

I easily located the farm of Lodas in the fork of the rivers, and circled low looking for a suitable landing place. As I did so, a number of men working in the fields dropped their tools and ran toward the house, from which several other persons came to observe the ship. Evidently we aroused much excitement, and when I finally landed several men came

45

cautiously toward me with weapons ready for any eventuality. I climbed down from the cockpit and advanced to meet them, holding my hands above my head to assure them that my intentions were friendly. When we were within speaking distance, I hailed them.

"Which of you is Lodas?" I asked.

They all halted and looked at one big fellow who was in the lead.

"I am Lodas," he replied. "Who are you? and what do you want of Lodas?"

"I have a message for you," I said, holding out the leather envelope.

He came forward rather hesitantly and took it from me. The others waited while he opened and read it.

"All right," he said finally, "come to the house with me."

"First I'd like to make my ship fast in a safe place," I told him. "Where would you suggest? It should be protected from the wind and be somewhere where it can be watched at all times."

He looked at it rather dubiously for a moment; then he shook his head. "I haven't a building large enough to hold it," he said, "but you can put it between those two buildings over there. It will be protected from the wind there."

I looked in the direction he indicated and saw two large buildings, probably barns, and saw that they would answer as well as anything he had to offer; so I taxied the ship between them, and with the help of Lodas and his fellows fastened it down securely.

"Let no one ever touch it or go near it," I cautioned Lodas.

"I think no one will wish to go near it," he said feelingly.

It must have looked like some monster from another world to those simple Amtorian rustics.

The ship tied down, the hands returned to the fields; and Lodas led me to the house, two women who had run out to enjoy the excitement accompanying us. The house, a long narrow building running east and west, had a verandah extending its full length on the south side and was windowless on the north, the side from which the prevailing warm winds came and the occasional hot blasts from the equatorial regions. Lodas led me into a large central room that was a combination living room, dining room, and kitchen. In addition to a huge fireplace there was a large clay oven, the former necessitated during the winter months when the colder winds came from the antarctic.

At the door of the room Lodas sent the women away, saying that he wished to speak with me alone. He seemed nervous and fearful; and when we were alone he drew me to a bench in a far corner of the room and sat close to me, whispering in my ear.

"This is bad business," he said. "There are spies everywhere. Perhaps some of the men working for me were sent by Mephis. He has spies spying upon everyone and spies spying upon spies. Already rumors have come from Amlot of a strange thing that flies through the air dropping death and fire upon the forces of Mephis. At once my workers will know that it is this thing that you came in. They will be suspicious; they will talk; if there is a spy among them he will get word to Mephis, and that will be the end of me. What am I to do?"

"What did the message tell you to do?" I asked.

"It told me to get you into Amlot; that was all."

"Are you going to do it?"

"I would do anything for Kord, my jong," he said simply. "Yes, I shall do it; but I shall probably die for it."

"Perhaps we can work out a plan," I suggested. "If there is a spy here or if your men talk too much, it will be as bad for me as for you. Is there any place near here where I could hide my ship—some place that it would be reasonably safe?"

"If Mephis hears of it, it will not be safe here," said Lodas, and I appreciated the truth of his statement. He thought for a moment; then he shook his head. "The only place that I can think of is an island off the coast just south of us."

"What sort of an island?" I asked. "Any clear, level land on it?"

"Oh, yes; it is a very flat island. It is covered with grass. No one lives there. It is seldom that anyone goes there—never since the revolution."

"How far off shore is it?"

"It lies very close. I row to it in a few minutes."

"You row to it? You have a boat?"

"Yes, once a year we row over to pick the berries that grow there. The women make jam of them that lasts all the rest of the year."

"Fine!" I exclaimed. "Now I have a plan that will remove all suspicion from you. Listen." For ten minutes I talked, explaining every detail of my scheme. Occasionally Lodas slapped his knee and laughed. He was hugely pleased and relieved. Lodas was a big, simple, good

47

natured fellow. One couldn't help but like and trust him. I didn't want to get him in any trouble, on his own account; and, too, I knew that any trouble I got him into I would have to share.

We decided to put my plan into execution immediately; so we left the house; and as we passed the women, Lodas spoke to me angrily.

"Get off my farm!" he cried. "I'll have nothing to do with you."

We went at once to the ship and cast off the ropes; then I taxied it out toward the field where I had landed. Lodas followed on foot, and when we were within earshot of some of the men, he shouted at me loudly. "Get out of here! I'll have nothing to do with you. Don't ever let me see you on my farm again." The farm hands looked on in wide-eyed amazement, that grew wider eyed as I took off.

As I had done when I took off from Sanara I flew in a direction opposite that I intended going; and when I was out of sight circled back toward the ocean. I found the island Lodas had described and landed easily. Some high bushes grew on the windward side, and behind these I made the ship fast. I worked on it until dark, and had it so securely fastened down that I didn't believe that anything short of a hurricane could blow it away.

I had brought a little food with me from Sanara; and, after eating, I crawled into the cabin and settled myself for the night. It was very lonely out there with only the wind soughing through the bushes and the surf pounding on the shore of that unknown sea. But I slept and dreamed of Duare. I knew that she must be worrying about me already, and I felt like a dog to have treated her so. I hoped that Muso would soon tell her that I had but gone on a mission for him. At the worst, I hoped to be home by the second day.

I awoke early and crossed the island to the shoreward side; and about half an hour later I saw a huge gantor approaching, drawing a wagon behind him. As he came nearer I recognized Lodas perched upon the animal's back. I waved to him, and he waved back. Leaving his conveyance near the shore, Lodas climbed down to a little cove, and presently I saw him pushing a crude boat into the water. Soon I was in it with him, and he was rowing back to the mainland.

"How did our little scheme work?" I asked him.

"Oh, fine," he said, with a broad grin. "I wouldn't tell them what you wanted me to do, but I told them that it was something wrong and that I was going to Amlot to tell the authorities about it. That satisfied them all; so if there was a spy among them I don't think he will give us any trouble. You are a very smart man to have thought of this plan."

Once in the cove, we pulled the boat up onto a little ledge and climbed up to the waiting conveyance, a four wheeled, boxlike cart loaded with hay and vegetables. Lodas forked some of the hay to one side and told me to lie down in the depression he had made; then he forked the hay back on top of me.

It was about ten miles to Amlot, and of all the uncomfortable ten miles I ever rode those took first prize. The hay was soft enough to lie on; but the seeds got in my ears and nose and mouth and under my harness and loincloth, and I almost suffocated beneath the pile of hay on top of me. The motion of the cart was eccentric, to say the least. It pitched and wobbled and bumped over a road that must have been new when longevity serum was invented, but never had a shot of it. The gait of the gantor was much faster than I had anticipated. He evidently had a long, swinging walk; and we must have made at least six miles an hour, which is somewhere between the speed of a horse's walk and trot.

But at last we got to Amlot. I knew that, when we came to a stop and I heard men's voices questioning Lodas. Finally I heard one say, "Oh, I know this farmer. He brings stuff into the city often. He's all right." They let us go on then, and I could tell by the sound of the wheels that we were rolling over a pavement. I was inside the walls of Amlot! I hoped the remainder of my mission would prove as readily fulfilled as this first part of it, and there was no reason to believe that it would not. If it did, I should be back with Duare by the following day.

We must have driven a considerable distance into the city before we stopped again. There was a short wait during which I heard voices; but they were low, and I could not overhear what was being said; then there was a creaking sound as of the hinges of a heavy gate, and immediately we moved forward a short distance and stopped again. Once more the hinges groaned, and then I heard Lodas's voice telling me to come out. I didn't need a second invitation. Throwing the hay aside, I stood up. We were in the courtyard of a one story house. A man was standing with Lodas looking up at me. He didn't seem very glad to see me.

"This is my brother, Horjan," said Lodas, "and, Horjan, this is—say, what is your name my friend?"

"Wasn't it in the message I brought?" I asked, pretending surprise.

"No, it wasn't."

Perhaps it would be as well, I thought, if I didn't publicize my true name too widely. "Where I come from," I said, "I would be called Homo Sapiens. Call me Homo;" so Homo I became.

"This is bad business," said Horjan. "If we are found out, the Zani Guard will come and take us off to prison; and there we shall be tortured and killed. No, I do not like it."

"But it is for the jong," said Lodas, as though that were ample reason for any sacrifice.

"What did the jong ever do for us?" demanded Horjan.

"He is our jong," said Lodas simply. "Horjan, I am ashamed of you."

"Well, let it pass. I will keep him this night, but tomorrow he must go on about his business. Come into the house now where I can hide you. I do not like it. I do not like it at all. I am afraid. The Zani Guard do terrible things to one whom they suspect."

And so I went into the house of Horjan in Amlot, a most unwelcome guest. I sympathized with the two brothers, but I could do nothing about it. I was merely obeying the orders of Muso.

VII: ZERKA

Horjan gave me a little room on the court and told me to stay there so that no one would see me; then he and Lodas left me. It was not long before Lodas returned to say that he was going to take his produce to market and then start home. He wanted to say goodby to me and wish me luck. He was a fine, loyal fellow.

The hours dragged heavily in that stuffy little room. At dusk Horjan brought me food and water. He tried to find out what I had come to Amlot for, but I evaded all his questions. He kept repeating that he would be glad to get rid of me, but at last he went away. After I had eaten I tried to sleep, but sleep didn't seem to want to come. I had just finally started to doze when I heard voices. They came from the adjoining room, and the partition was so thin that I could hear what was said. I recognized Horjan's voice, and there was the voice of another man. It was not Lodas.

"I tell you it is bad business," Horjan was saying. "Here is this man about whom I know nothing. If it is known that he is hiding here I shall get the blame, even though I don't know why he is hiding."

"You are a fool to keep him," said the other.

"What shall I do with him?" demanded Horjan.

"Turn him over to the Zani Guard."

"But still they will say that I had been hiding him," groaned Horjan.

"No; say that you don't know how he got into your house—that you had been away, and when you came back you found him hiding in one of your rooms. They will not harm you for that. They may even give you a reward."

"Do you think so?" asked Horjan.

"Certainly. A man who lives next to me informed on a neighbor, and they gave him a reward for that."

"Is that so? It is worth thinking about. He may be a dangerous man. Maybe he has come to assassinate Mephis."

"You could say that that was what he came for," encouraged the other.

"They would give a very big reward for that, wouldn't they?" asked Horjan.

"Yes, I should think a very big reward."

51

There was silence for several minutes; then I heard a bench pushed back. "Where are you going?" demanded Horjan's visitor.

"I am going to tell the Zanis," said Horjan.

"I shall go with you," announced his companion. "Don't forget that the idea is mine—I should have half the reward. Maybe two-thirds of it."

"But he is my prisoner," insisted Horjan. "It is I who am going to notify the Zani Guard. You stay here."

"I rather guess not. If I told them what I know, they would arrest you both; and I'd get a great big reward."

"Oh, you wouldn't do that!" cried Horjan.

"Well, I certainly shall if you keep on trying to rob me of the reward."

"Oh, I wouldn't rob you of it. I'll give you ten per cent."

The other laughed. "Ten per cent nothing. *I'll* give *you* ten per cent—and that's much more than you deserve—plotting against Mephis and Spehon and the rest of them."

"You can't put that over on me," shouted Horjan. "Nobody'll believe you anyhow. Everybody knows what a liar you are. Hey, where are you going? Come back here! I'm the one that's going to tell them."

I heard the sound of running feet, the slamming of a door, and then silence. That was my cue to get out of there, and I can tell you that I didn't waste any time acting on it. I didn't know how far they'd have to go to find a member of the Zani Guard. There might be one at the next corner for all that I knew. I found my way out of the house in short order, and when I reached the avenue my two worthy friends were still in sight, quarrelling as they ran. I turned and melted into the shadows of the night that fell in the opposite direction.

There was no use running. I didn't even hurry, but sauntered along as though I were an old resident of Amlot going to call on my mother-in-law. The avenue I was in was dark and gloomy, but I could see a better lighted one ahead; so I made for that. I passed a few people, but no one paid any attention to me. Presently I found myself in an avenue of small shops. They were all open and lighted, and customers were coming and going. There were lots of soldiers on the street, and here I caught my first sight of a member of the Zani Guard.

There were three of them together, and they were swaggering down the sidewalk elbowing men, women and children into the gutter. I felt a little nervous as I approached them, but they paid no attention to me.

I had been doing a great deal of thinking since I had overheard the conversation between Horjan and his accomplice. I couldn't forget that the latter had linked Spehon's name with that of Mephis. The message that I carried in my pocket was addressed to Spehon. What could Muso be communicating secretly with a leader of the Zanis for? It didn't make sense, and it didn't sound good. It worried me. Then I recalled the inexplicable secrecy of my departure and the fact that Muso had warned me against telling Lodas the name of the person I was bearing a message to. Why was he afraid to have that known? and why had he been so relieved when he assured himself that I could not read Amtorian? It was a puzzle that was commencing to clear itself up in my mind, or at least I was beginning to suspect something of the solution. Whether I were right or not, I might never know; or I might learn it tomorrow. That depended largely upon whether or not I delivered the message to Spehon. I was almost minded to try to get out of the city and back to my ship; then fly to Sanara and lay the whole matter before Taman, whom I trusted. But my sometimes foolish sense of duty to a trust imposed in me soon put that idea out of my head. No, I would go on and carry out my orders—that was my duty as a soldier.

As I proceeded along the avenue the shops took on a more prosperous appearance, the trappings and jewels of the people on the street became richer. Gorgeously trapped gantors carried their loads of passengers to and fro or stopped before some shop while master or mistress entered to make a purchase. Before one brilliantly lighted building twenty or thirty huge gantors waited. When I came opposite the building, I looked in. It was a restaurant. The sight of the bright lights, the laughing people, the good food attracted me. The meager meal that Horjan had brought me had only served to whet my appetite. I entered the building, and as I did so I saw that it was apparently filled to capacity. I stood for a moment looking about for a vacant table, and was about to turn and walk out when an attendant came up to me and asked me if I wished to dine. I told him I did, and he led me to a small table for two where a woman was already seated.

"Sit here," he said. It was a trifle embarrassing.

"But this table is occupied," I said.

"That is all right," said the woman. "You are welcome to sit here."

There was really nothing else for me to do but thank her and take the vacant chair. "This is very generous of you," I said.

"Not at all," she assured me.

"I had no idea, of course, that the attendant was bringing me to someone else's table. It was very presumptuous of him."

She smiled. She had a very lovely smile. In fact she was a very good looking woman; and, like all the civilized women of Amtor that I had seen, apparently quite young. She might have been seventeen or seven hundred years old. That is what the serum of longevity does for them.

"It was not so presumptuous as it might seem," she said; "at least not on the part of the attendant. I told him to fetch you."

I must have looked my surprise. "Well, of course, that was very nice of you," was the only banality I could think of at the moment.

"You see," she continued, "I saw you looking for a table, there was a vacant chair here, I was alone and lonely. You don't mind, do you?"

"I'm delighted. You were not the only lonely person in Amlot. Have you ordered?"

"No; the service here is execrable. They never have enough attendants, but the food is the best in town. But of course you have eaten here often—everyone eats here."

I didn't know just what position to take. Perhaps it would be better to admit that I was a stranger rather than pretend I was not and then reveal the fact by some egregious error that I would be certain to make in conversation with any person familiar with Amlot and the manners and customs of its people. I saw that she was appraising me closely. Perhaps it would be more correct to say inventorying me—my harness, my other apparel, my eyes. I caught her quizzical gaze upon my eyes several times. I determined to admit that I was a stranger when our attention was attracted to a slight commotion across the room. A squad of Zani Guards was questioning people at one of the tables. Their manner was officious and threatening. They acted like a bunch of gangsters.

"What's all that about?" I asked my companion.

"You don't know?"

"It is one of the many things I don't know," I admitted.

"About Amlot," she concluded for me. "They are looking for traitors and for Atorians. It goes on constantly in Amlot nowadays. It is strange you have never noticed it. Here they come now."

Sure enough, they were heading straight across the room for our table, and their leader seemed to have his eyes on me. I thought then that he was looking for me in particular.

Later I learned that it is their custom to skip around a place, examining a few people in each. It is more for the moral effect on the citizens than for anything else. Of course they do make arrests, but that is largely a matter of the caprice of the leader unless a culprit has been pointed out by an informer.

The leader barged right up to me and stuck his face almost into mine. "Who are you?" he demanded. "Give an account of yourself."

"He is a friend of mine," said the woman across the table. "He is all right, kordogan."

The man looked at her, and then he wilted. "Of course, Toganja," he cried apologetically; then he marched his men away and out of the restaurant.

"Perhaps it was very well for me, in addition to having your company, that this was the only vacant chair in the restaurant; although I really had nothing to fear. It is just disconcerting for a stranger."

"Then I guessed correctly? You are a stranger?"

"Yes, Toganja; I was about to explain when the kordogan pounced on me."

"You have credentials though?"

"Credentials? Why, no."

"Then it is very well for you that I was here. You would certainly have been on your way to prison now and probably shot tomorrow—unless you have friends here."

"Only one," I said.

"And may I ask who that one is?"

"You." We both smiled.

"Tell me something about yourself," she said. "It doesn't seem possible that there is such an innocent abroad in Amlot today."

"I just reached the city this afternoon," I explained. "You see, I am a soldier of fortune. I heard there was fighting here, and I came looking for a commission."

"On which side?" she asked.

I shrugged. "I know nothing about either side," I said.

"How did you get into the city without being arrested?" she demanded.

"A company of soldiers, some workers, and a few farmers were coming through the gate. I just walked through with them. Nobody stopped me; nobody asked me any questions. Did I do wrong?"

She shook her head. "Not if you could get away with it. Nothing is wrong that you can get away with. The crime is in getting caught. Tell me where you are from, if you don't mind."

"Why should I mind? I have nothing to conceal. I am from Vodaro." I remembered having seen a land mass called Vodaro on one of Danus's maps. It extended from the southern edge of the south temperate zone into the terra incognita of the antarctic. Danus said that little was known of it. I hoped that nothing was known of it. Nothing less than I knew of it could be known.

She nodded. "I was sure you were from some far country," she said. "You are very different from the men of Korva. Do all your people have grey eyes?"

"Oh, yes, indeed," I assured her. "All Vodaroans have grey eyes, or nearly all." It occurred to me that she might meet a Vodaroan some day who had black eyes. If she got to inquiring around right in this restaurant she might find one. I didn't know, and I wasn't taking any chances. She seemed to be quite an alert person who liked to seek after knowledge.

An attendant finally condescended to come and take our order, and after the dinner arrived I found that it was well worth waiting for. During the meal she explained many things about conditions in Amlot under the rule of the Zanis, but so adroit was she that I couldn't tell whether she was a *phile* or a *phobe*. While we were in the midst of dinner another detachment of the Zani Guard entered. They went directly to a table next to us where a citizen who accompanied them pointed out one of the diners.

"That is he," he cried accusingly. "His great-grandmother was nursed by an Atorian woman."

The accused rose and paled. "Mistal!" cried the kordogan in charge of the detachment, and struck the accused man heavily in the face, knocking him down; then the others jumped on him and kicked and beat him. Finally they dragged him away, more dead than alive. (A *mistal* is a rodent about the size of a cat. The word is often used as a term of opprobrium, as one might say "Pig!").

"Now what was all that about?" I asked my companion. "Why should a man be beaten to death because his great-grandmother nursed at the breast of an Atorian woman?"

"The milk and therefore the blood of an Atorian entered the veins of an ancestor, thereby contaminating the pure blood of the super race of Korva," she explained.

"But what is wrong with the blood of an Atorian?" I asked. "Are Atorians diseased?"

"It is really rather difficult to explain," she said. "If I were you I should just accept it as fact while in Amlot—and not discuss it."

I realized that that was excellent advice. From what I had seen in Amlot I was convinced that the less one discussed anything the better off he would be and the longer he would live.

"You haven't told me your name," said the Toganja; "mine is Zerka."

I couldn't safely give her my own name, and I didn't dare use Homo any longer because I was sure I had been reported by Horjan and his good friend; so I had to think of another name quickly.

"Vodo," I said quickly, thinking that Vodo of Vodaro sounded almost colossal.

"And in your own country you must be a very important man," she said. I could see she was trying to pump me, and I saw no use in saying I was a street car conductor or an author or anything like that. They wouldn't sound important enough; and, anyway, as long as I was launched on a career of deception I might as well make a good job of it.

"I am the Tanjong of Vodaro," I told her, "but please don't tell anyone. I'm travelling incognito." A tanjong is the son of a ruling jong—a prince.

"But how in the world did your government ever permit you to travel alone like this? Why, you might be killed."

"From what I have seen of Amlot I can readily agree with you," I said, laughing. "As a matter of fact, I ran away. I got tired of all the pomp and ceremony of the court. I wanted to live my life as a man."

"That is very interesting," she said. "If you want to take service here, perhaps I can help you. I am not without influence. Come and see me tomorrow. The driver of any public gantor knows where my palace is. Now I must be going. This has been quite an adventure. You have kept me from utter boredom."

I noticed that she said utter.

I walked to the door with her, where two warriors saluted her and followed us to the curb, one of them summoning the driver of a gantor—her private conveyance.

"Where do you stop?" she asked me, as she waited for her gantor.

"I haven't stopped yet," I told her. "You know I am a stranger here. Can you suggest a good place?"

"Yes, come with me; I'll take you there."

The ornate howdah on the broad back of her gantor seated four in the front compartment—two and two, facing one another; behind this was another seat where the two armed guards rode.

As the great beast strode majestically along the avenue, I watched with interest the night life of this Amtorian city. Previously I had been in Kooaad, the tree city of Vepaja, in the Thorist city of Kapdor, in Kormor, the city of the dead, and in lovely Havatoo. The latter and this city of Amlot were, of all of them, the only cities in the true sense of the word; and while Amlot could not compare with Havatoo, it was yet a city of life and activity. Though the hour was late, this main avenue was thronged with people; lines of gaily caparisoned gantors moved in both directions carrying their loads of passengers gay and laughing, grave and serious. Everywhere the Zani Guardsmen were in evidence, their strange headdress distinguishing them from all others—a two-inch ridge of hair from forehead to nape. Their apparel was distinctive too, because of its ornateness. Shops and restaurants, gambling houses and theaters, brilliantly lighted, lined the avenue. Amlot did not seem like a city at war. I mentioned this to Zerka.

"It is our way of keeping up the morale of the people," she explained. "As a matter of fact, the last war, which brought on the revolution, left us disillusioned, bitter, and impoverished. We were compelled to give up our entire navy and merchant marine. There was little life and less laughter on the avenues of Amlot; then, by decree of Kord, the jong, every public place was required to reopen and the people, in some instances, actually driven into the streets to patronize them. The effect was electrical, and after the revolution the Zanis encouraged the practice. It has been most helpful in maintaining the spirit of the people. Well, here we are at the travellers' house. Come and see me tomorrow."

I thanked her for her courtesy to me and for the pleasant evening she had given me. The driver had placed the ladder against the gantor's side, and I was about to descend, when she laid a hand on my arm. "If you are questioned," she said, "tell them what you told me; and if they do not believe you, or you get in any trouble, refer them to me. Tell them I have given you permission to do so. Here, take this and wear it," and she slipped a ring from one of her fingers and handed it to me; "it will substantiate your claim to my friendship. And now, one other thing. I would not mention again that you are a tanjong. Royalty is not so popular in Amlot as it once was; why, is immaterial. A very great jong came here recently in search of an only daughter who had been kidnaped. He is still imprisoned in the Gap kum Rov—if he is yet alive."

A very great jong whose only daughter had been kidnaped! Could it be possible?

"What great jong is that?" I asked.

Her eyes narrowed a little as she replied, "It is not well to be too inquisitive in Amlot during these times."

"I am sorry," I said; then I descended to the sidewalk, and her great gantor moved off down the avenue.

VIII: MUSO'S MESSAGE

The travellers' house, or hotel, to which Zerka had brought me was really quite magnificent, indicating that Amlot had been a city of considerable wealth and importance in this part of Amtor. The lobby served the same purpose that a lobby in an Earthly hotel does. The desk was a large, circular booth in the center. There were benches, chairs, divans, flowers; small shops opened from it. I felt almost at home. The lobby was crowded. The ubiquitous Zani Guard was well represented. As I stepped to the desk, two of them followed me and listened while the clerk questioned me, asking my name and address.

"Where are your credentials?" barked one of the Zanis.

"I have none," I replied. "I am a stranger from Vodaro, seeking military service here."

"What! No credentials, you mistal? You are probably a dog of a spy from Sanara." He bellowed so loud that the attention of everyone in the lobby was attracted, and all about us there fell a silence that seemed to me the silence of terror. "This is what you need," he yelled, and struck at me. I am afraid I lost my temper, and I know I did a very foolish thing. I parried his blow and struck him heavily in the face—so heavily that he sprawled backward upon the floor fully ten feet from me; then his companion came for me with drawn sword.

"You had better be sure what you are doing," I said, and held out the ring Zerka had given me so that he could see it.

He took one look at it and dropped the point of his weapon. "Why didn't you say so?" he asked, and his tone was very different from what that of his fellow had been. By this time the latter had staggered to his feet and was trying to draw his sword. He was quite groggy.

"Wait," his companion cautioned him, and went and whispered in his ear, whereupon they both turned and left the lobby like a couple of whipped dogs. After that the clerk was the personification of courtesy. He inquired about my luggage, which I told him would arrive later; then he called a strapping porter who had a chairlike contraption strapped to his back. The fellow came and knelt before me and I took my seat in the chair, for it was obvious that that was what was expected of me; then he stood up, took a key from the clerk and ran up three flights of stairs with me—a human elevator, and the only sort of elevator known to Amlot. The fellow was a veritable composite of Hercules and Mercury. I tried to tip him after he had set me down in my room, but he couldn't understand my good intentions. He thought I was trying to bribe him to do something that he shouldn't do. I am sure he reported me as a suspicious character after he returned to the desk.

My room was large and well furnished; a bath opened from it. A balcony in front overlooked the city out to the ocean, and I went out there and stood for a long time thinking over all that had occurred to me, but mostly thinking of Duare. I also thought much on my strange encounter with the Toganja Zerka. I couldn't quite convince myself that her interest in me was wholly friendly, yet I really had no reason to doubt it; except, perhaps, that she seemed a woman of mystery. It is possible that I doubted her sincerity because of my own deceitfulness; yet what else could I have done? I was in an enemy city, where, if the truth about me were even suspected, I should have received short shrift. As I could not tell the truth, I had to lie; and while I was lying, I might as well make a good job of it, I reasoned. I was sure that I had completely deceived her. Had she also deceived me? I knew the city was full of spies. What better way to entice a stranger into unwary admissions than through a beautiful woman—it is as old as espionage itself.

The possibility that Duare's father, Mintep, might be a prisoner here gave me the most concern and resolved me to remain until I had definitely established the truth or falsity of my suspicions. The reference to Spehon, made by Horjon's companion, that linked closely with the leader of Zanism the name of the man to whom I bore a message from Muso was also good for considerable conjecture. I was frankly apprehensive that all was not as it should be. There was a way to discover, perhaps. I took the leather envelope containing Muso's message from my pocket pouch, broke the seals, and opened it. This is what I read:

Muso, the Jong,

Addresses Spehon at Amlot.

May success attend your ventures and old age never overtake you.

Muso dispatches this message to Spehon by Carson of Venus, who cannot read Amtorian.

If Sanara were to fall into the hands of Mephis, this unfortunate civil war would be ended.

That would be well if Muso were to be jong of Korva after the fall of

Sanara.

If Mephis wishes all this to happen, let three blue rockets be shot into the air before the main gate of Sanara on three successive nights.

On the fourth night let a strong force approach the main gate secretly, with stronger reserves held nearby; then Muso will cause the main gates to be thrown open for the purpose of permitting a sortie. But there will be no sortie. The troops of Mephis may then enter the city in force. Muso will surrender, and the bloodshed may cease.

Muso will make a good jong, conferring always with Mephis.

The Zanis shall be rewarded.

It would be regrettable, but best, if Carson of Venus were destroyed in Amlot.

May success be yours.

Muso

Jong

I turned a little cold at the thought of how near I had been to delivering that message without reading it. I hadn't realized that I had been carrying my death warrant around on me as innocently as a babe in the woods. I looked around for some means of destroying it, and found a fireplace in one corner of the room. That would answer the purpose nicely. I walked to it, carrying the document; and, taking my little pocket fire-maker from my pouch, was about to set fire to it when something caused me to hesitate. Here was a valuable document—a document that might mean much to Taman and to Korva if it were properly utilized. I felt that it should not be destroyed, yet I didn't like the idea of carrying it around with me. If I could but find a hiding place! But where? No place in this room would answer if I were even slightly under suspicion, and I knew that I already was. I was positive that the moment I left the room it would be thoroughly searched. I put the message back in its leather container and went to bed. Tomorrow I would have to solve this problem; tonight I was too tired.

I slept very soundly. I doubt that I moved all night. I awoke about the 2nd hour, which would be about 6:40 A.M. Earth time. The Amtorian day is 26 hours, 56 minutes, 4 seconds of Earth time. Here it is divided into thirty-six hours of forty minutes each, the hours being numbered from 1 to 36. The 1st hour corresponds roughly with mean sunrise, and is about 6 A.M. Earth time. As I rolled over and stretched for a moment before arising, I felt quite content with myself. I was to call on Zerka this very morning with the possibility of obtaining service of some nature with the Zanis that might make it possible for me to ascertain if Mintep were really in Amlot. I had read Muso's message to Spehon; so that that was no longer a menace to me. My only real problem now was to find a suitable hiding place for it, but I have so much confidence in myself that I did not apprehend any great difficulty in doing so.

Stepping out of bed, I walked to the balcony for a breath of fresh air and a look at the city by daylight. I saw that the travellers' house stood much closer to the waterfront than I had imagined. There was a beautiful landlocked harbor lying almost at my feet. Innumerable small boats lay at anchor or were moored to quays. They were all that the enemy had left to the conquered nation.

A new day was before me. What would it bring forth? Well, I would bathe, dress, have breakfast, and see. As I crossed to the bath, I saw my apparel lying in disorder on the floor. I knew that I had not left it thus, and immediately I became apprehensive. My first thought, naturally, was of the message; and so the first thing that I examined was my pocket pouch. The message was gone! I went to the door. It was still locked as I had left it the night before. I immediately thought of the two Zani Guardsmen with whom I had had an altercation in the lobby. They would have their revenge now. I wondered when I would be arrested. Well, the worst they could do would be to take me before Spehon, unless he had already issued orders for my destruction. If I were not immediately arrested, I must try to escape from the city. I could not serve Mintep now by remaining. My only hope was to reach Sanara and warn Taman.

I performed my toilette rather perfunctorily and without interest; then I descended to the lobby. It was almost empty. The clerk on duty spoke to me quite civilly, for a hotel clerk. No one else paid any attention to me as I found the dining room and ordered my breakfast.

I had made up my mind that I was going to see Zerka. Maybe she could and would help me to escape from the city. I would give her a good reason for my wishing to do so. After finishing my breakfast, I returned to the lobby. The place was taking on an air of greater activity. Several members of the Zani Guard were loitering near the desk. I determined to bluff the whole thing through; so I walked boldly toward them and made some inquiry at the desk. As I turned away, I saw two more of the guardsmen enter the lobby from the avenue. They were coming directly toward me, and I at once recognized them as the two with whom I had had the encounter the preceding night. This, I thought, is the end. As they neared me both of them recognized me; but they passed on by me, and as they did so, both saluted me. After that I went out into the street and window shopped to kill time; then about the 8th hour (10:40 A.M. E.T.) I found a public gantor and directed the driver to take me to the palace of Toganja Zerka. A moment later I was in the cab of my amazing taxi and lumbering along a broad avenue that paralleled the ocean.

Shortly after we left the business portion of the city we commenced to pass magnificent private palaces set in beautiful grounds. Finally we stopped in front of a massive gate set in a wall that surrounded the grounds of one of these splendid residences. My driver shouted, and a warrior opened a small gate and came out. He looked up at me questioningly.

"What do you want?" he asked.

"I have come at the invitation of the Toganja Zerka," I said.

"What is your name, please?" he asked.

"Vodo," I replied; I almost said Homo.

"The Toganja is expecting you," said the warrior as he threw open the gates.

The palace was a beautiful structure of white marble, or what looked like white marble to me. It was built on three sides of a large and beautiful garden, the fourth side being open to the ocean, down to the shore of which the flowers, shrubbery, and lawn ran. But just then I was not so much interested in scenic beauty as I was in saving my neck.

After a short wait, I was ushered into the presence of Zerka. Her reception room was almost a throne room, and she was sitting in a large chair on a raised dais which certainly carried the suggestion of sovereignty. She greeted me cordially and invited me to sit on cushions at her feet.

"You look quite rested this morning," she observed. "I hope you had a good night."

"Very," I assured her.

"Any adventure after I left you? You got along all right in the hotel?"

I had a feeling she was pumping me. I don't know why I should have, unless it was my guilty conscience; but I did.

"Well, I had a little altercation with a couple of the Zani Guardsmen," I admitted; "and I lost my temper and knocked one of them down—very foolishly."

"Yes, that was foolish. Don't do such a thing again, no matter what the provocation. How did you get out of it?"

"I showed your ring. After that they left me alone. I saw them again this morning, and they saluted me."

"And that was all that happened to you?" she persisted.

"All of any consequence."

She looked at me for a long minute without speaking. She seemed either to be weighing something in her mind or trying to fathom my thoughts. Finally she spoke again. "I have sent for a man to whom I am going to entrust your future. You may trust him implicitly. Do you understand?—implicitly!"

"Thank you," I said. "I don't know why you are doing these things for me, but I want you to know that I appreciate your kindness to a friendless stranger and that if I can serve you at any time—well, you know you have only to command me."

"Oh, it is nothing," she assured me. "You saved me from a very bad evening with myself, and I am really doing very little in return."

Just then a servant opened the door and announced: "Maltu Mephis! Mantar!"

A tall man in the trappings and with the headdress of a Zani Guardsman entered the room. He came to the foot of the dais, saluted and said, "Maltu Mephis!"

"Maltu Mephis!" replied Zerka. "I am glad to see you, Mantar. This is Vodo," and to me, "This is Mantar."

"Maltu Mephis! I am glad to know you, Vodo," said Mantar.

"And I am glad to know you, Mantar," I replied.

A questioning frown clouded Mantar's brow, and he glanced at Zerka. She smiled.

"Vodo is an utter stranger here," she said. "He does not yet understand our customs. It is you who will have to inform him."

Mantar looked relieved. "I shall start at once," he said. "You will forgive me, then, Vodo, if I correct you often?"

"Certainly. I shall probably need it."

"To begin with, it is obligatory upon all loyal citizens to preface every greeting and introduction with the words Maltu Mephis. Please, never omit them. Never criticize the government or any official or any member of the Zani Party. Never fail to salute and cry Maltu Mephis whenever you see and hear others doing it. In fact, it will be well if you always do what you see everyone else doing, even though you may not understand."

"I shall certainly follow your advice," I told him; but what my mental reservations might be I wisely kept to myself, as he probably did also.

"Now, Mantar," said Zerka, "this ambitious young man is from far Vodaro, and he wishes to take service as a soldier of Amlot. Will you see what you can do for him? And now you must both be going, as I have many things to attend to. I shall expect you to call and report to me occasionally, Vodo."

IX: I Become a Zani

Mantar took me immediately to the palace formerly occupied by the Jong, Kord, and now by Mephis and his lieutenants. "We shall go directly to Spehon," he said. "No use wasting time on underlings."

To Spehon! To the man whom Muso had advised to destroy me! I felt positive that the message must already be in his hands, as it must have been stolen by Zani spies who would have delivered it to him immediately, was going to my doom.

"Why do we go to Spehon?" I asked.

"Because he is head of the Zani Guard, which also includes our secret police. Zerka suggested that I find you a berth in the Guard. You are fortunate indeed to have such a friend as the Toganja Zerka; otherwise, if you had been given service at all, it would have been at the front, which is not so good since Muso enlisted the services of this fellow called Carson of Venus with his diabolical contrivance that flies through the air and rains bombs on everyone."

"Flies through the air?" I asked, in simulated surprise. "Is there really such a thing? What can it be?"

"We really don't know much about it," Mantar admitted. "Of course everyone at the front has seen it, and we learned a little from some prisoners we took who were members of a Sanaran party making a sortie against our first line. They told us the name of the fellow who flies it and what little they knew of him and of the thing he calls an anotar, but that really was not much. Yes, you will be fortunate if you get into the Guard. If you are an officer, it is something of a sinecure; but you'll have to watch your step. You must hate everything we Zanis hate and applaud everything that we applaud, and under no circumstances must you ever even look critical of anything that is Zani. To demonstrate what I mean: We were listening to a speech by Our Beloved Mephis one evening, when a bright light shining in his eyes unexpectedly caused one of my fellow officers to knit his brows and half close his eyes in what appeared to be a frown of disapproval. He was taken out and shot."

"I shall be very careful," I assured him, and you may believe me that I meant it.

The palace of the former jong was, indeed, a magnificent structure; but I'm afraid I didn't fully appreciate it as I walked through its corridors toward the office of Spehon—my mind was on other things. We arrived at last at a waiting room just outside the office of the great man, and there we waited for about half an hour before we were summoned into the presence. Men were coming and going to and from the waiting room in a constant stream.

66

It was a very busy place. Most of them wore the Zani uniform and sported the Zani coiffure, and as they came and went the air was filled with "Maltu Mephises" and Zani salutes.

At last we were ushered into the presence of Spehon. Like nearly all civilized Amtorians, he was a handsome man; but his mouth was a shade too cruel and his eyes a little too shifty for perfection. Mantar and I each said "Maltu Mephis" and saluted; Spehon said "Maltu Mephis! Greetings, Mantar. What brings you here?" He barked the words like a human terrier.

"Maltu Mephis! This is Vodo," announced Mantar. "I bring him to you at the suggestion of the Toganja Zerka, his good friend. She recommends him for a commission in the Guard."

"But he is not even a Zani," expostulated Spehon.

"He is not even from Anlap," said Mantar, "but he wishes to be a Zani and serve Our Beloved Mephis."

"From what country do you come?" demanded Spehon.

"From Vodaro," I replied.

"Have you any Atorian blood in your veins?"

"Had I, I should have been killed in Vodaro," I cried.

"And why?" he asked.

"And why, may I ask, Spehon, do *you* kill Atorians?" I demanded.

"Naturally, because they have large ears," he replied "We must keep the blood of Korvans pure."

"You have answered your own question, Spehon," I told him. "We Vodaroans are very proud of our pure blood; so we, too, kill the Atorians because they have large ears."

"Excellent!" he exclaimed. "Will you swear to love, honor, and obey Our Beloved Mephis, give your life for him, if necessary, and hold him and the Zani Party above all else?"

"I swear!" I said, but I had my fingers crossed; then we all saluted and said, "Maltu Mephis!"

"You are now a Zani," he announced. He saluted me, and said, "Maltu Mephis!"

"Maltu Mephis!" I said, and saluted him.

"I appoint you a tokordogan," said Spehon, saluting, "Maltu Mephis!"

"Maltu Mephis!" I replied, and saluted. A tokordogan is somewhat similar to a lieutenant. A kordogan is comparable to a sergeant and as the prefix to means either high or over, my title might be translated as oversergeant.

"You will be responsible for Vodo's training," Spehon told Mantar; then we all Maltu Mephised and saluted.

I breathed a sigh of relief as I quitted the office of Spehon. Evidently he had not received the message as yet. I still had a little lease on life.

Mantar now took me to the officers' quarters adjoining the barracks of the Zani Guard, which are situated close to the palace; and here a barber gave me an approved Zani haircut, after which I went with Mantar to be outfitted with the regulation uniform and weapons of a tokordogan of the Zani Guard.

On the way back from the outfitters I heard a great commotion ahead of us on the broad avenue along which we were walking. People lining the curbs were shouting something that I could not understand at first, but presently recognized as the incessant chant of the Zanis—Maltu Mephis! As the sound approached I saw that the shouts were being directed at a procession of giant gantors.

"Our Beloved Mephis comes this way," said Mantar. "When he approaches, stand at salute and shout Maltu Mephis as loud as you can until he has passed."

Presently I saw men standing on their heads in the street and along the curbs, and each of them was shouting Maltu Mephis at the top of his lungs. Only the women and the members of the Zani Guard did not stand on their heads; but everybody shouted, and everybody saluted who was not using his hands to keep him from falling down. They commenced when the first elephant came within a few yards of where they stood, and continued until the last elephant had passed them by the same distance. They all seemed absolutely devoid of any sense of humor.

When the procession came abreast of me I saw such ornately housed and trapped gantors as I had never before seen. In the gilded howdah of one of them sat a small, insignificant looking man in the uniform of a Zani kordogan. It was Mephis. He looked actually frightened; and his eyes were constantly darting from side to side, warily. I guessed, what I learned later, that he was in mortal fear of assassination—and with good reason.

After Mephis had passed I expressed a wish to Mantar to see something of the city. I told him that I would especially like to go down to the waterfront and look at the boats there. Immediately he was suspicious. I have never seen such suspicious people.

"Why do you want to go down to the waterfront?" he asked.

"We Vodaroans depend much on the sea for most of our food; therefore we are all familiar with boats and fond of them. I am naturally interested in seeing the design of the small boats of Anlap. As a matter of fact, I should like much to own one. I like to sail and fish."

My explanation seemed to satisfy him, and he suggested that we hail a passing gantor and ride down to the quay, which we did. I saw innumerable boats, most of which had evidently not been in use for some considerable time. Mantar explained that they probably belonged to men who were serving at the front.

"Do you suppose I could buy or rent one of them?" I asked.

"You do not have to buy or rent anything," he said. "You are now a member of the Zani Guard and can take anything you please from anyone who is not a member of the Guard." That was an excellent convention—for the Zani Guardsmen.

Having seen and learned what I had come to the waterfront for, I was ready to return into the city and commence my real training under Mantar. This lasted in an intensive form for about a week, during which time I did not visit Zerka nor receive any call from Spehon. Could it be that the message had not come into his hands? I could scarcely believe it. Perhaps, I thought, he is not going to accept Muso's offer and is not, therefore, interested in destroying me. But that line of reasoning was not wholly satisfactory. Knowing how suspicious they were and vindictive, I could not believe that Spehon would permit me to live or wear the uniform of a Zani Guardsman a day after he discovered how I had lied to him. I was compelled to consider the matter only as a wholly baffling mystery.

I cannot say that I enjoyed the companionship of my fellow officers, with the exception of Mantar. He was a gentleman. Most of the others were surly boors—an aggregation of ignorant thugs, bums, and gangsters. The men under us were of the same types. All seemed suspicious of one another, and I think especially of Mantar and me. They resented the fact that we were cultured; and the very fact that we were cultured seemed to feed their suspicions of us; and because they felt their inferiority, they hated us, too. Because of this atmosphere of suspicion it was difficult for me to learn anything about the one thing that kept me from escaping from Amlot at once—I refer to my belief that Mintep might be a prisoner in the city. I felt that I could easily escape by commandeering a small boat and sailing along the coast until I came to the island where my ship was hidden, but first I must assure myself of the truth or falsity of my suspicion. All that I might learn was what I overheard by accident. I could not ask direct questions nor reveal undue interest in any political or other controversial matter. As a result, my nerves were under constant strain, so watchful must I be of every word or act or even facial expression or tone of voice. But it was like that with everyone else—I think even with Spehon and perhaps with Mephis himself, for every man knew that a spy or an informer was watching to pounce upon him at his first mis-step. The result was not conducive to garrulity—conversation, as such, did not exist except between occasional intimates; and even then I doubt that men dared speak what was in their hearts.

Ten days had passed, and I was no nearer my goal than on the day I arrived in Amlot. I was worried and was grieving over Duare. What must she think? Had Muso told her? Was she well? These unanswerable questions nearly drove me mad. They almost convinced me that I should abandon my self-imposed commission and return to Sanara, but when I thought of the happiness it would bring to Duare were she to be reunited with her father or her grief were she to know that he might be a prisoner in Amlot and in constant danger of being destroyed, I could only remain and do what I considered my duty. I was in such a mood when I received an invitation from Zerka to visit her. It was a welcome relief, and I went with pleasure.

We greeted each other with the usual "Maltu Mephis!" which, for some reason, seemed wholly out of place and incongruous between us. I always had a feeling that Zerka was hiding a laugh about something, and especially so when we went through the silly flubdub of Zani ritual. Hers was a most engaging personality that seemed to me to be wholly out of harmony with the stupidities of Zanism.

"My!" she exclaimed with a little laugh, "what a handsome Zani Guardsman we make."

"With this haircut?" I demanded, making a wry face.

She put a finger to her lips. "Ssh!" she cautioned. "I thought that you would have learned better than that by this time."

"Mayn't I even criticize myself?" I asked, laughing.

She shook her head. "Were I you, I should criticize only Atorians and the enemy in Sanara."

"I don't even do that," I said. "I am what would be called in my wor—country a rubber stamp."

"That is a word I do not know," she said. "Can it be possible that the Vodaroans do not speak the same language as we?"

"Oh no; we speak the same language," I assured her.

"And read it, too?" she inquired.

"Why, of course."

"I thought so," she mused.

I couldn't imagine why she had thought otherwise, or why the matter was of any importance. Before I could ask her she veered off onto another track. "Do you like Mantar?" she asked.

"Very much," I said. "It is nice to have the companionship of one gentleman at least."

"Be careful," she cautioned again. "That is indirect criticism, but I can assure you it may be just as fatal. You needn't worry about me, however; I caution you only because there are always spies. One never may know who may be listening intently to his conversation in addition to the one to whom it is addressed. Suppose we go for a ride; then we can talk, and you can say anything you wish to. My driver has been with my family all his life. He would never repeat anything he heard."

It seemed a little strange that she should be encouraging me to talk openly, in view of the fact that she had previously warned me against it.

"I'm sure," I said, "that all the world might listen to what I have to say. I am most happy here."

"I am glad of that," she said.

"I have learned though that it is just as well not to talk too much. In fact, I am surprised that I have not forgotten how to talk."

"But of course you talk freely with Mantar?" she asked.

"I do not talk at all about anything I am not supposed to talk about," I said.

"But with Mantar, it is different," she urged. "You may trust him fully. Discuss anything you wish with him. Mantar would never betray you."

"Why?" I asked bluntly.

"Because you are *my* friend," she replied.

"I appreciate all that that implies," I said, "and am very grateful for your friendship. I wish that I might repay the obligation in some way."

"Perhaps you may have the chance some day—when I know you better."

A gantor was brought into the courtyard of the palace, and we mounted to the howdah. This time there were no armed guards—only ourselves and the driver.

"Where shall we go?" asked Zerka.

"Anywhere. I should like to see some more of the public buildings." I hoped in this way to discover the location of the Gap kum Rov, where the mysterious jong was imprisoned. I hadn't dared ask anyone; and I didn't dare ask Zerka, for notwithstanding her assurances that I might speak freely to her, I was not so sure that it would be wise. As far as I knew she might be a spy herself. The sudden friendship that she had fostered between us gave some color to this suspicion. I didn't want to believe it, for she seemed very sincere in her liking for me; but I could take no chances. I must suspect everyone. In that, I was becoming a true Zani.

She gave some directions to the driver; then she settled back. "Now," she said, "that we are comfortable and alone let's have a good talk. You see we really know very little about one another."

"I have wondered a great deal about you," I said. "You are such an important person, and yet you waste your time on a total stranger."

"I do not feel that I am wasting my time," she said. "It is not a waste of time to make new friends. I really have very few, you know. The war and the revolution took most of them—the war took my man." She said ooljagan—loveman. "I have lived alone ever since—rather a useless life, I am afraid. Now tell me about yourself."

"You know all there is to tell," I assured her.

"Tell me of your life in Vodaro," she insisted. "I should like to know something of the customs and manners of the people of that far country."

"Oh, I'm sure you wouldn't be interested. We are a simple people." I couldn't very well tell her that she probably knew more about Vodaro than I.

"But I would be interested," she insisted. "Tell me how you got here."

I was most uncomfortable. I feel that I am not a very convincing liar. This was really my first essay at really spectacular lying, and I was very much afraid that I might trip myself up. If I lied too much, I should have too many lies to remember. I already had enough to tax my memory as it was. My recollection of even the location of Vodaro was rather hazy. The country was shown on a map I had seen in the library of Danus at Kooaad. I remembered that fact concerning it; and that was about all, except that it was supposed to run far back into Karbol, the cold country.

I had to answer Zerka's question, and my explanation of how I got to Amlot would have to be uncheckable. It was necessary to do a lot of thinking in a split second.

"One of our merchants had chartered a small ship and had loaded it with furs with which he expected to trade for merchandise in foreign countries. We sailed north for a month without encountering land until we sighted Anlap. Here we were overtaken by a terrific storm which wrecked the ship. I was washed ashore, the sole survivor. A kindly farmer took me in, and from him I learned that I was in the Kingdom of Korva, on Anlap. He also told me about the war raging here, and brought me as far as the city gates with a load of farm produce. The rest, I have told you."

"And what was the name of this kindly farmer?" she asked, "He should be rewarded."

"I never learned his name," I said.

She looked at me with the oddest expression that made me feel that she knew I was lying; but perhaps it was only my guilty conscience that suggested that fear. Anyway, she didn't say anything more about the matter, for which I was deeply grateful. As we approached one of the main avenues of the city, I saw men standing on their heads shouting "Maltu Mephis!" and others saluting and shouting the same stereotyped mandatory laudative.

"Our Beloved Mephis must be abroad," I said.

She shot me a quick glance, but I maintained a perfectly serious demeanor. "Yes," she said, "and don't forget to stand up and salute and acclaim him. There is to be a review of troops outside the city. A new unit is going to the front. Our Beloved Mephis is on his way to review them now. Would you be interested in seeing it?"

I told her that I would; so after Mephis's cortege passed, we fell in behind and followed it out onto the plain beyond the city. After Mephis had taken his place and the shouting had died out and men had stopped standing on their heads, Zerka directed our driver to move to a point where we could watch the ceremonies advantageously. A large body of troops was massed at some distance to the left, and at a signal from Mephis, transmitted by trumpet to the waiting troops, they broke into column of companies and advanced toward the great man so that they would pass before him at the proper distance. It was so similar to the passing in review of troops in civilized countries on Earth that it was rather startling; but when I gave the matter thought, I could not conceive any more practical way of reviewing troops.

When the first company was at about a hundred yards from Mephis, the step was changed. The entire company, in unison, took three steps forward, hopped once on the left foot, took three more steps forward, leaped straight up to a height of about two feet, and then repeated. They continued in this way until they had passed a hundred yards beyond Mephis; and all the time they shouted "Maltu Mephis!" in a sing-song chant.

"Is that not impressive?" demanded Zerka, at the same time watching me carefully as though to detect my exact reaction.

"Very," I said.

"It is an innovation sponsored by Our Beloved Mephis," explained Zerka.

"I could easily imagine that that might be so," I replied.

X: THE PRISON OF DEATH

I had enjoyed my long visit with Zerka. We had eaten again at the same restaurant in which we had met, we had gone to one of the amazing theaters of Amlot, and we had finally gotten home about the nineteenth hour, which would be about 2:00 A.M. Earth time; then Zerka had invited me in for a little supper. But during all that time neither one of us had learned anything of importance about the other, which I think was the uppermost desire in the mind of each of us; nor had I had the Gap kum Rov pointed out to me. However, I had had a rather enjoyable day, marred only by my constant and depressing worries concerning Duare.

The theaters of Amlot and the plays shown therein under the Zanis are, I believe, of sufficient interest to warrant a brief digression. The audiences in the theaters sit with their backs, toward the stage. In front of them on the end wall of the theater is a huge mirror, so placed that every one in the house may see it, just as a motion picture screen is placed in our cinemas. The action taking place on the stage behind the audience is reflected from the mirror, and by a system of very ingenious lighting stands out brilliantly. By manipulation of the lights the scenes may be blacked out completely to denote a lapse of time or permit a change of scenery. Of course the reflections of the actors are not life size, and therefore the result gives an illusion of unreality reminiscent of puppet shows or the old days of silent pictures. I asked Zerka why the audience didn't face the stage and look directly at the actors; and she explained that it was because the profession of acting had formerly been in disrepute, and it had been considered a disgrace to be seen upon a stage. They got around it in this ingenious way; and it was considered extremely poor form to turn around and look directly at the actors, even though the profession was now considered an honorable one.

But the thing that amused me most was the play. There are one hundred theaters in Amlot, and the same play was being shown in all of them. It was the life of Mephis! Zerka told me that it consisted of one hundred and one episodes, each episode constituting a night's performance, and that it was absolutely obligatory on all citizens to attend the theater at least once in every ten days. They were given certificates to attest that they had done so. The play had already been running for more than a year. Mephis's publicity agent should have been born in Hollywood.

The day following my visit with Zerka I was given a detachment of the Zani Guard and told to report to the Gap kum Rov. It was just as easy as that. Here I had been trying to locate the place for days, and without success; now I was being officially detailed to the prison. Just what my duties were to be and whether I was to remain there or not, I did not know. My orders were simply to report to one Torko, governor of the prison—The Prison of Death.

My detachment consisted of eleven men, one of whom was a kordogan, whom I ordered to march the detachment to the prison. I didn't wish them to know that I had no idea where it was. The prison stood on a small island in the bay, not more than a hundred yards off shore. I had seen it on several occasions, but had not guessed that it was the notorious Gap kum Rov. At the quay we entered a small launch belonging to the prison and were soon standing beneath its grim walls. The mere fact that we were members of the Zani Guard gave us immediate entrance, and I was presently in the office of Torko. He was a large man, heavy of feature and coarse, with one of the crudest human faces I have ever seen. Unlike most Amtorians, he was ill-favored. His manner was gruff and surly, and I sensed immediately that he did not like me. Well, our dislike was mutual.

"I never saw you before," he growled, after I had reported. "Why didn't they send someone I knew? What do *you* know about running a prison?"

"Nothing," I assured him. "I didn't ask for the assignment. If I can put up with it, I guess you can."

He grunted something I couldn't understand, and then said, "Come with me. Now that you're here, you've got to familiarize yourself with the prison and with my system of administration."

A second door in his office, opposite the one through which I had entered, opened into a guardroom full of Zani Guardsmen, one of whom he ordered to go to the courtyard and fetch my men; then he crossed to another door, heavily bolted and barred. When this was opened it revealed a long corridor on either side of which were partitions of heavy iron bars back of which were huddled several hundred prisoners, many of whom were covered with wounds and sores.

"These mistals," explained Torko, "have been guilty of disrespect to Our Beloved Mephis or to the glorious heroes of the Zani Guard. Show them no mercy."

Next he took me to the end of the corridor, through another door, and up a flight of stairs to the second floor, where there were two rows of individual cells, each cell containing from one to three prisoners, although each would have been cramped quarters for one.

"These are traitors," said Torko. "They are awaiting trial. We really haven't enough room here; so every day, when we receive a new batch, we take some of them out and shoot them. Of course, we give them a chance to confess first. If they do, why naturally a trial isn't necessary; and we shoot them. If they don't confess, we shoot them for impeding justice."

"Very simple," I commented.

"Very," he agreed, "and eminently fair, too. It was my idea."

"Our Beloved Mephis knows how to choose his lieutenants, doesn't he?"

He looked very pleased at that, and really smiled. It was the first time I had seen him smile, and I hoped he wouldn't do it again—his smile seemed only to make his face appear more cruel and repulsive.

"Well," he exclaimed, "I guess I was wrong about you—you talk like a good man and an intelligent one. We shall get along splendidly. Are you very close to Our Beloved Mephis?"

"I'm sorry to say that I'm not," I told him. "I merely serve him."

"Well, you must know someone who is," he insisted.

I was about to reply, telling him that I was afraid I knew no one who had the ear of Mephis, when he caught sight of the ring hanging on a chain around my neck. It was too small to fit on any of my fingers; I wore it thus.

"I should say you do know someone close to Mephis," he exclaimed. "The Toganja Zerka! Man! but are you lucky!"

I did not reply, as I had no stomach to discuss Zerka with this beast; but he insisted. "She was bright to come over to the Zanis," he said. "Most of her kind were killed; and those that did come over are usually under suspicion, but not Toganja Zerka. They say Mephis has the utmost confidence in her and often consults her in matters of policy. It was her idea to have the Zani Guard patrol the city constantly looking for traitors and beating up citizens who couldn't give a good account of themselves. Playing the life of Our Beloved Mephis constantly in all the theaters was also her idea, as was that of having civilians stand on their heads and cheer whenever Our Beloved Mephis passed. Even the expression Our Beloved Mephis was coined by her. Oh, she's a brilliant one. Mephis owes her a lot."

All this was most illuminating. I had always felt that Zerka applauded Mephis with her tongue in her cheek. I had even doubted her loyalty to him or to the Zani cause. Now I didn't know what to think, but I certainly congratulated myself upon the fact that I had not confided in her. Somehow, I felt a little sad and depressed, as one does when disillusioned, especially if the disillusionment concerns a friend he has admired.

"Now," continued Torko, "if you should put in a good word for me with the toganja, it would be sure to reach the ear of Our Beloved Mephis. How about it, my excellent friend?"

"Wait until I know you better," I said; "then I shall know what to report to the toganja." This was almost blackmail, but I felt no compunction.

"You'll have nothing but the best to report of me," he assured me; "we shall get along splendidly. And now I'll take you down to the courtroom where the trials are conducted and show you the cells where Our Beloved Mephis keeps his favorite prisoners."

He led me down into a dark basement and into a large room with a high bench running across one end. Behind the bench were a number of seats, the whole being raised a couple of feet above the floor level. Around the sides of the room were low benches, which evidently served as seats for spectators. The rest of the room was devoted to an elaborate display of the most fiendish instruments of torture the mind of man might conceive. I shall not dwell upon them. It is enough to say that all were horrible and many of them absolutely unmentionable. All my life I shall be trying to forget them and the hideous things I was forced to see perpetrated there upon both men and women.

Torko made a wide, sweeping gesture, proudly. "These are my pets," he said. "Many of them are my own invention. Believe me, just a look at them usually gets a confession; but we give them a taste of them anyway."

"After they have confessed?" I asked.

"Why certainly. Is it not a treasonable thing to cheat the state of the usefulness of these ingenious contrivances that have cost so much in thought and money to produce?"

"Your logic is unimpeachable," I told him. "It is evident that you are a perfect Zani."

"And you are a man of great intelligence, my friend, Vodo. And now, come with me—you shall see some more of this ideal plant."

He led me into a dark corridor beyond the torture chamber. Here were small cells, feebly illuminated by a single dim light in the central corridor. A number of men were confined, each in a cell by himself. It was so dark that I could not distinguish the features of any of them, as all remained in the far corners of their cramped quarters; and many sat with their faces hidden in their hands, apparently oblivious of the fact that we were there. One was moaning; and another shrieked and gibbered, his mind gone.

"That one," said Torko, "was a famous physician. He enjoyed the confidence of everyone, including Our Beloved Mephis. But can you imagine how heinously he betrayed it?"

"No," I admitted, "I cannot. Did he attempt to poison Mephis?"

"What he did was almost as bad. He was actually apprehended in the act of alleviating the agony of an Atorian who was dying of an incurable disease! Can you imagine?"

"I am afraid," I said, "that my imagination is permanently incapacitated. There are things that transcend the limits of a normal imagination. Today you have shown me such things."

"He should have been executed; but when he went mad, we felt that he would suffer far more if he lived. We were right. We Zanis are always right."

"Yes," I agreed, "it is the indisputable privilege of all Zanis to be always right."

He took me next down a dark corridor to another room at the far side of the building. There was nothing here but an enormous furnace and a foul odor.

"Here is where we burn the bodies," Torko explained; then he pointed to a trap door in the floor. "Be careful not to step on that," he cautioned. "It is not very substantial. We dump the ashes down there into the bay. The chute is quite large. If the door gave way with you, you'd land in the bay."

I spent a week undergoing a sort of training in inhumanity; and then Torko obtained a leave of absence, and I was left in charge as acting governor of the Prison of Death. During the time that he was away I did what I could to alleviate the sufferings of the inmates of that hideous sink of misery and despair. I permitted them to clean up their foul cells and themselves, and I gave them quantities of good food. There were no "trials" while I was in charge and only one execution, but that was ordered by a higher authority—in fact, by Mephis himself. I received word about the 11th hour one day that Mephis would visit the prison at the 13th hour—2:00 P.M. E.T. As I had never met the great man and had no idea how to receive him or conduct myself, I was in something of a quandary; as I knew that a single error, however unintentional, would affront him and result in my execution. At last it occurred to me that my kordogan might help me out. He was more than anxious to display his knowledge; and so, as the 13th hour approached, I anticipated the coming event with considerable assurance. With a number of warriors as an escort, I waited at the quay with the prison launch; and when Mephis hove in sight with his retinue, I lined up my men and we saluted and Maltu Mephised him in orthodox style. He was quite affable as he greeted me with condescending cordiality.

"I have heard of you," he said. "If you are a protege of Toganja Zerka, you must be a good Zani."

"There is only one good Zani," I said.

He thought I meant him; and he was pleased. The kordogan had the remaining guardsmen lined up in the guard room; and as we passed through, every one saluted and shouted "Maltu Mephis!" at the top of his voice. I wondered at the time how Mephis could listen to such forced acclaim without feeling like the ass he was; but I suppose an ass doesn't mind being an ass, or doesn't realize it.

The great man asked to be taken into the basement, where his own particular prisoners were incarcerated. He took only me and two of his aides with him, one of the latter being his present favorite—an effeminate looking man, bejeweled like a woman. When we

79

reached the room where the prisoners' cells were located, Mephis directed me to show him the cell of Kord, the former jong of Korva.

"Torko has not told me the names of any of these prisoners," I explained. "He said it was your wish that they remain nameless."

Mephis nodded. "Quite right," he said, "but of course the acting governor of the prison should know who they are—and keep the knowledge to himself."

"You wish to speak to me, Mephis?" asked a voice from a nearby cell.

"That is he," said Mephis. "Unlock his cell."

I took the master key from my belt and did as Mephis bid me.

"Come out!" commanded he.

Kord was still a fine looking man, though wasted by confinement and starvation. "What do you want of me?" he demanded. There was no "Maltu Mephis!" here, no cringing. Kord was still the jong, and Mephis shrunk in his presence to the insignificant scum he had been born. I think he felt it; for he commenced to bluster and talk loud.

"Drag the prisoner to the courtroom!" he shouted to me, and turned back to that room himself, followed by his aides.

I took Kord gently by the arm. "Come," I said.

I think he had expected to be jerked or kicked, as he probably had been on former occasions, for he looked at me in something of surprise when I treated him with decent consideration. My heart certainly went out to him, for it must have been galling to a great jong such as he had been to be ordered about by scum like Mephis; and, too, there must have been the knowledge that he was probably going to be tortured. I expected it, and I didn't know how I was going to be able to stand and watch it without raising a hand in interference. Only my knowledge that it would have done him no good and resulted in my own death and, consequently, the defeat of all my own plans, convinced me that I must hide my indignation and accept whatever was forthcoming.

When we entered the courtroom, we saw that Mephis and his aides had already seated themselves at the judges' bench, before which Mephis directed me to bring the prisoner. For a full minute the dictator sat in silence, his shifty eyes roving about the room, never meeting those of Kord and myself but momentarily. At last he spoke.

"You have been a powerful jong, Kord," he said. "You may be jong once more. I have come here today to offer you your throne again."

He waited, but Kord made no reply. He just stood there, erect and majestic, looking Mephis squarely in the face, every inch a king. His attitude naturally irritated the little man, who, though all-powerful, still felt his inferiority to the great man before him.

"I tell you, I will give you back your throne, Kord," repeated Mephis, his voice rising. "You have only to sign this," and he held up a paper. "It will end needless bloodshed and restore Korva the peace and prosperity she deserves."

"What is written on the paper?" demanded Kord.

"It is an order to Muso," replied Mephis, "telling him to lay down his arms because you have been restored as jong and peace has been declared in Korva."

"Is that all?" asked Kord.

"Practically all," replied Mephis. "There is another paper here that you will sign that will insure the peace and prosperity of Korva."

"What is it?"

"It is an order appointing me advisor to the jong, with full power to act in his place in all emergencies. It also ratifies all laws promulgated by the Zani Party since it took control of Korva."

"In other and more candid words, it betrays my few remaining loyal subjects into the hands of Mephis," said Kord. "I refuse, of course."

"Just a moment," snapped Mephis. "There is another condition that may cause you to alter your decision."

"And that?" inquired Kord.

"If you refuse, you will be considered a traitor to your country, and treated accordingly."

"Assassinated?"

"Executed," corrected Mephis.

"I still refuse," said Kord.

Mephis rose from his seat. His face was livid with rage. "Then die, you fool!" he almost screamed; and, drawing his Amtorian pistol, poured a stream of the deadly r-rays into the defenseless man standing before him. Without a sound, Kord, Jong of Korva, sank lifeless to the floor.

XI: THE NET DRAWS CLOSER

The next day, as I was making my rounds of the prison, I took it upon myself to inquire of a number of the prisoners as to the nature of the offenses that had resulted in such drastic punishment, for to be imprisoned in Gap kum Rov was, indeed, real punishment. I found that many of them had expressed their opinions of Mephis and the Zanis too freely, and that supposed friends had informed upon them. Many did not know what the charges against them were, and quite a few were there because of old grudges held against them by members of the Zani Guard. One man was there because an officer of the Zani Guard desired his woman; another because he had sneezed while, standing upon his head, he should have been shouting Maltu Mephis. The only hope any of them had of release was through bribery or the influence of some member of the Zani Party, but this latter was difficult to obtain because of the fear the Zanis themselves felt of directing suspicion upon themselves. These inquiries I had made were of the prisoners in the big tanks on the main floor. My interest lay in the dim corridors below ground, where I thought that Mintep might be confined. I had not dared reveal any interest in these prisoners for fear of directing suspicion upon myself, for I knew that there were constantly informers among the prisoners, who won favors and sometimes freedom by informing upon their fellow prisoners. Torko had told me that I was not even to know the names of the prisoners on that lower level; but I was determined to learn if Mintep was among them, and finally I hit upon a plan that I hoped would serve my purpose. With difficulty, I wrote some very bad verse in Amtorian, which I sang to a tune that had been popular in America when I left the Earth. In two of the verses was the message I wished to use to elicit a sign from Mintep that he was a prisoner there, and thus to locate his cell.

To allay suspicion, I formed the habit of singing my song as I went about my daily duties; but I sang it at first only on the upper floors. My kordogan and some of the other members of the guard showed an interest in my song, and asked me questions about it. I told them that I didn't know the origin or significance of it, that the words meant nothing to me, and that I only sang it because I was fond of the tune.

In addition to my essay at poetry, I had been busy along another line of endeavor. The cell and door locks of the prison were not all alike, but there was a master key which opened any of them. In Torko's absence, I carried this master key; and one of the first things I did after it came into my possession was to take it into the city and have two duplicates made. I had no definite plan in mind at the time wherein they might figure; but, though I took considerable risk in having them made, I felt that eventually they must be of the utmost value in releasing Mintep, if it developed that he was a prisoner in Gap kum Rov.

You can scarcely realize the caution I was forced to observe in everything that I did, in order not to arouse suspicion, to incur enmities, or engender envy, for every citizen of Amlot was a spy or a potential informer. Yet I had to make haste, for I knew that over my head hung constantly that Damoclean message from Muso. Who had it? Why had they not struck?

I was accustomed to wandering around the prison alone, inspecting the cells, the guardroom, the kitchen; so it would arouse no comment were I discovered anywhere; and the fact that I was almost constantly humming or singing my foolish song was, I felt, evidence that there was nothing irregular or surreptitious about my activities.

It was the day before Torko's return that I determined to try to ascertain definitely if Mintep were imprisoned at the lower level. With this idea in mind, I went singing through the prison, feeling, as usual, like a loony. Down to the basement I went, through the courtroom, and into the dim precincts of the forbidden cells. I went to the furnace and passed along the corridor where the cells were, and there I sang the two verses that I had written to arouse Mintep's interest and, perhaps, beguile an acknowledgement, if he were there. These are the verses to which I refer, roughly translated into English:

"Mourned by a nation,

"By her kinsman sought,

"Duare lives, and

"Of thy fate knows naught.

"A word, a sign, is

"All she asks of thee.

"If thou canst give it,

"Put thy trust in me."

I kept right on singing other verses, or humming the air, as I passed along the cells; but there was no response. Clear to the end of the corridor I went, and then turned back. Once more I sang those two verses, and as I approached the last cells, I saw a man pressing close to the bars of one of them. In the dim light, I could not see his features plainly; but as I

83

passed close to him, he whispered the single word, "Here." I noted the location of his cell and continued on my way.

With Torko, I occupied my office next to the guardroom: and when I arrived there, I found my kordogan waiting with some new prisoners. One of my duties was to receive all prisoners, question them, and assign them to cells. A clerk kept a record of all such matters. All I was supposed to do, according to Torko, was to insult and browbeat the prisoners.

There were three of them, and they lined them up in front of my desk. As I looked up at them, I immediately recognized one of them as Horjan, the brother of Lodas; and, to my horror, I saw recognition slowly dawn in his eyes; or at least I thought I did.

"What is your name?" I asked.

"Horjan," he replied.

"Why are you here?"

"Some time ago I reported a stranger hiding in my home," he replied. "When the guard came, they found no one—the man had escaped. They were very angry with me. A neighbor, whom I had told of my discovery of the man, became angry with me; and today he went to the Zani Guard and told them that he had seen the man and that I had been hiding him, and that I only reported the matter because I knew that he would. He told them that the man was a spy from Sanara and that he was still in the city."

"How does he know the man is still in the city?" I demanded.

"He says that he has seen him—that he could never forget his face or his *eyes*—he says that the man was wearing *the uniform of an officer of the Zani Guard*."

I knew that Horjan's friend had not seen me, and that this was merely Horjan's way of communicating to me the fact that he had recognized me.

"It would be too bad if your friend bore false witness against an officer of the Zani Guard," I said. "If anyone did that, it would be necessary to torture him before killing him. But perhaps it would be well to question your friend to learn if *he* ever did see this man in your house, and have him describe him."

Horjan paled. He realized that he had committed an error; and he was terrified, for he knew that his friend had never seen me and could not describe me.

"I hope it does not get him in trouble," I continued. "It is deplorable that there should be so much loose talking in Amlot. It would be better if some people held their tongues."

"Yes," said Horjan, meekly, "there is too much loose talk; but you may rest assured that I shall never talk."

I hoped that he meant it, but I was very much concerned. Now, indeed, must I take immediate steps to escape from Amlot. But how? My problem was now further complicated by my discovery of Mintep.

On the following day Torko returned, and I was sent to make an arrest in the quarter occupied by scholars and scientists. There were many Amtorians living in this quarter, for their minds incline toward scholarly pursuits and scientific investigation. Here the few who had not been killed were segregated, not being allowed to leave the quarter, which, because of them, was in bad repute with the Zanis, who wreaked mean little persecutions on the slightest pretext. The Zanis hated scholars and scientists, as they hated all who were superior to them in any way.

On my way to the quarter, I passed a field where hundreds of boys were being drilled by kordogans of the Zani Guard. There were little fellows of five and six and many older boys. This same thing was going on all over Amlot—this was the only schooling the Zani boys received. The only toys they were allowed to have were weapons. Babes in arms were given blunt daggers upon which to cut their teeth. I said that was all the schooling they received. I was wrong. They were taught to shout "Maltu Mephis!" upon any pretext or upon none; and a chapter from *The Life of Our Beloved Mephis*, written by himself, was read to them daily. It was quite a comprehensive education—for a Zani.

The quarter where I was to make the arrest had formerly been a prosperous one, as, during the regime of the jongs, scholars and scientists were held in high esteem; but now it was run down, and the few people I saw on the streets looked shabby and half starved. Arrived at the home of my victim (I can think of nothing more suitable to call him) I walked in with a couple of my men, leaving the others outside. As I entered the main room, which might be called the living room, I saw a woman step hurriedly between some hangings at the opposite side of the room; but not so quickly but that I recognized her. It was Zerka.

A man and woman sitting in the room rose and faced me. They both looked surprised; the woman, frightened. They were exceptionally fine looking, intelligent appearing people.

"You are Narvon?" I asked of the man.

He nodded. "I am Narvon. What do you want of me?"

"I have orders to place you under arrest," I said. "You will come with me."

"What is the charge against me?" he asked.

"I do not know," I told him. "I have orders to arrest you—that is all I know."

He turned sadly to say goodby to the woman; and as he took her in his arms and kissed her, she broke down. He choked a little as he tried to comfort her.

The kardogan who accompanied me stepped forward and seized him roughly by the arm. "Come on!" he shouted gruffly. "Do you think we are going to stand here all day while you two dirty traitors blubber?"

"Leave them alone!" I ordered. "They may say goodby."

He shot me an angry look, and stepped back. He was not my own kardogan, who, while bad enough, had learned from me to temper his fanaticism a little with tolerance if not compassion.

"Well," he said, "while they're doing that, I'll search the house."

"You'll do nothing of the kind," I said. "You'll stay here and keep still and take your orders from me."

"Didn't you see that woman sneak into the back room when we entered?" he demanded.

"Of course I did," I replied.

"Ain't you going to go after her?"

"No," I told him. "My orders were to arrest this man. I had no orders to search the house or question anyone else. I obey orders, and I advise you to do the same."

He gave me a nasty look, and grumbled something I did not catch; then he sulked for the remainder of the day. On the way back to the prison I walked beside Narvon; and when I saw that the kardogan was out of earshot, I asked him a question in a whisper.

"Was the woman I saw in your house, the one who ran out of the room as I came in, a good friend of yours?"

He looked just a bit startled, and he hesitated a fraction of a second too long before he replied. "No," he said. "I never saw her before. I do not know what she wanted. She came in just ahead of you. I think she must have made a mistake in the house, and been embarrassed and confused when you came in. You know it is often dangerous, nowadays, to make mistakes, however innocent they may be."

He could have been tortured and executed for a statement such as that, and he should have known it. I cautioned him.

"You are a strange Zani," he said. "You act almost as though you were my friend."

"Forget it," I warned him.

"I shall," he promised.

At the prison I took him at once to Torko's office.

"So you are the great scholar, Narvon," snarled Torko. "You should have stuck to your books instead of trying to foment a rebellion. Who were your accomplices?"

"I have done nothing wrong," said Narvon; "and so I had no accomplices in anything that was wrong."

"Tomorrow your memory will be better," snapped Torko. "Our Beloved Mephis himself will conduct your trial, and you will find that we have ways in which to make traitors tell the truth. Take him to the lower level, Vodo; and then report back here to me."

As I passed through the courtroom with Narvon, I saw him pale as his eyes took in the instruments of torture there.

"You will not name your accomplices, will you?" I asked.

He shuddered and seemed to shrink suddenly. "I do not know," he admitted. "I have never been able to endure pain. I do not know what I shall do. I only know that I am afraid—oh, so terribly afraid. Why can they not kill me without torturing me!"

I was very much afraid, myself—afraid for Zerka. I don't know why I should have been— she was supposed to be such a good Zani. Perhaps it was the fact that she had run away from men in the uniform of the Zani Guard that aroused my suspicions. Perhaps it was because I had never been able to reconcile my belief in her with the knowledge that she was a Zani. Quite a little, too, because Narvon had so palpably tried to protect her.

When I returned to Torko's office, the kardogan who had been with me when I made the arrest was just leaving. Torko was scowling ominously.

"I have heard bad reports of your conduct during my absence," he said.

"That is strange," I said—"unless I have made an enemy here; then you might hear almost anything, as you know."

"The information has come from different sources. I am told that you were very soft and lenient with the prisoners."

"I was not cruel, if that is what is meant," I replied. "I had no orders to be cruel."

"And today you did not search a house where you knew a woman to be hiding—the home of a traitor, too."

"I had no orders to search the house or question anybody," I retorted. "I did not know the man was a traitor; I was not told what his offense had been."

"Technically, you are right," he admitted; "but you must learn to have more initiative. We arrest no one who is not a menace to the state. Such people deserve no mercy. Then you whispered with the prisoner all the way to the prison."

I laughed outright. "The kardogan doesn't like me because I put him in his place. He became a little insubordinate. I will not stand for that. Of course I talked with the prisoner. Was there anything wrong in that?"

"The less one talks with anyone, the safer he is," he said.

He dismissed me then; but I realized that suspicions were aroused; and there was that brother of Lodas just full of them, and of real knowledge concerning me, too; and primed to spill everything he knew or suspected at the first opportunity. Whatever I was going to do, I must do quickly if I were ever going to escape. There were too many fingers ready to point at me, and there was still the message from Muso. I asked permission to go fishing the next day; and as Torko loved fresh fish, he granted it.

"You'd better stay around until after Our Beloved Mephis has left the prison," he said. "We may want your help."

The next day Narvon was tried before Mephis, and I was there with a detail of the guard—just ornamentally. We lined up at attention at each end of the bench where Mephis, Spehon, and Torko sat. The benches at the sides of the room were filled with other Zani bigwigs. When Narvon was brought in, Mephis asked him just one question.

"Who were your accomplices?"

"I have done nothing, and I had no accomplices," said Narvon. He looked haggard and his voice was weak. Every time he looked at an instrument of torture he winced. I saw that he was in a state of absolute funk. I couldn't blame him.

Then they commenced to torture him. What I witnessed, I would not describe if I could. It beggars description. There are no words in any language to depict the fiendishly bestial cruelties and indignities they inflicted on his poor, quivering flesh. When he fainted, they resuscitated him; and went at it again. I think his screams might have been heard a mile away. At last he gave in.

"I'll tell! I'll tell!" he shrieked.

"Well?" demanded Mephis. "Who are they?"

"There was only one," whispered Narvon, in a weak voice that could scarcely be heard.

"Louder!" cried Mephis. "Give him another turn of the screw! Then maybe he'll speak up."

"It was the Toganja Z—" Then he fainted as they gave the screw another turn. They tried to revive him again, but it was too late—Narvon was dead.

XII: Hunted

I went fishing; and I caught some fish, but I couldn't forget how Narvon died. I shall never forget it. Nor could I forget his dying words. Coupled with what I had seen in his house, I knew the name that had died in his throat. I wondered if any of the Zanis there had guessed what I *knew*. Not only did I fish, but I did some reconnoitering and a great deal of thinking. I wondered what to do about Zerka. Should I risk Mintep's life to warn her, with considerable likelihood that I might be arrested with her? Really, there was but one answer. I must warn her, for she had befriended me. I sailed around close to the prison, for there were certain things I must know about the outside of the place. I knew all that was necessary about the inside. After satisfying myself on the points concerning which I had been in doubt, I came ashore, and went to my quarters in the barracks. Here I found an order relieving me of duty at the prison. I guess Torko had found me too soft for his purposes; or was there something else, something far more sinister behind it? I felt a net closing about me.

As I sat there in my quarters with this most unpleasant thought as my sole company, a guardsman came and announced that the commandant wished me to report to him at once. This, I thought, is the end. I am about to be arrested. I contemplated flight; but I knew how futile such an attempt would be, and so I went to the commandant's office and reported.

"A dozen prisoners have been brought from the front at Sanara," he said. "I am detailing twelve officers to question them. We can get more out of them if they are questioned separately. Be very kind to the man you question. Give him wine and food. Tell him what a pleasant life a soldier may have serving with the armies of the Zanis, but get all the information you can out of him. When they have all been questioned, we shall turn them over to some private soldiers to entertain for a few days; then we shall send two of them back to the front and let them escape to tell about the fine treatment they received in Amlot. That will mean many desertions. The other ten will be shot."

The Zanis were full of cute little tricks like that. Well, I got my man and took him to my quarters. I plied him with food, wine, and questions. I wanted to know about Sanara on my own account, but I didn't dare let him know how much I knew about the city and conditions there. I had to draw him out without him suspecting me. It chanced that he was a young officer—a nice chap, well connected. He knew everyone and all the gossip of the court and the important families.

There were certain questions that it would be quite natural for any Zani to ask. Those relative to the defenses of the city and other military matters he answered glibly—so glibly that I knew he was lying, and I admired him for it. When I asked him about Muso, he talked freely. It was evident that he didn't like Muso.

"He's turned his woman out," he volunteered. "Her name is Illana. She is a fine woman. Everyone is very much incensed over it, but what can anyone do? He is jong. The woman he has selected in Illana's place does not want to take it. It is common talk that she loathes Muso; but he is jong, and if he orders her to come, she will have to come, because she has no man. He was killed here in Amlot. Muso sent him here on a dangerous mission. Everyone believes that he sent him to his death purposely."

I felt myself turning cold. The next question on my lips withered in my dry mouth. I made two attempts before I could utter an intelligible sound.

"Who was this man?" I asked.

"He was the man who used to fly over your lines and drop bombs on you," he replied. "His name was Carson of Venus—odd name."

I had asked my last question of that man. I took him out and turned him over to the soldiers who were to entertain the prisoners; then I hastened toward the quay. It was already dark, and the street I chose was not well lighted. That was the reason I chose it. I had almost reached the quay, when I ran into a detachment of the Zani Guard in command of an officer. The latter hailed me from the opposite side of the street; then he crossed toward me, leaving his detachment behind.

"I thought I recognized you," he said. It was Mantar. "I have an order for your arrest. They are scouring the city for you."

"I have been in my quarters. Why didn't they look there?"

"Torko said you had gone fishing."

"Why am I being arrested?" I asked.

"They think you are a Sanaran spy. A prisoner named Horjan informed on you. He said he found you hiding in his house just the day before you applied for a commission in the Guard."

"But Zerka?" I asked. "Won't they suspicion her? It was she who sponsored me."

"I had thought of that," he said.

"Well, what are you going to do with me?" I asked. "Are you going to turn me in?"

"I wish you would tell me the truth," he said. "I am your friend; and if what Zerka and I have suspected for long is true, I will help you."

I recalled that Zerka had told me I could trust this man implicitly. I was lost anyway. They had enough against me to torture and murder me. Here was a straw. I clutched it.

"I am Carson of Venus," I said. "I came here with a message for Spehon from Muso. It was stolen from me."

"Where were you going when I stopped you?" he asked.

"I was going back to Sanara, where my friends and my heart are," I told him.

"Can you get there?"

"I think I can."

"Then go. It is fortunate for you that none of my detail knew Vodo by sight. Good luck!" He turned and crossed the street, and I went on toward the quay. I heard him say to his kardogan. "He says that Vodo is in his quarters at the barracks. We shall go there."

I reached the quay without further incident, and found the same boat I had used for fishing earlier in the day and on several other occasions. It was a small boat with a single sail, scarcely more than a canoe. As I put off, I heard the sound of running feet along the quay; and then I saw men approaching.

A voice cried, "Stop! Come back here!" but I set my sail and got under way; then I heard the staccato br-r-r of r-rays, and a voice crying, "Come back here, Vodo! You can't get away."

For reply I drew my own pistol and fired back at them. I knew that that would disconcert their aim and give me a better chance to escape with my life. Long after I could no longer see them, they stood there firing out into the night.

I thought of Mintep with regret, but there was something far more precious at stake than his life or that of any man. I cursed Muso for his duplicity, and prayed that I might reach Sanara in time. If I did not, I could at least kill him; and that I promised to do.

Presently I heard the sound of a launch behind me, and knew that I was being pursued. Inside the harbor the breeze was light and fitful. If I couldn't reach the open sea ahead of my pursuers, I should have to depend upon eluding them in the darkness. In this I might be successful, or I might not. I couldn't hope to outdistance a launch even with a good wind, and about my only hope was to escape detection until I was able to discern from the sound of the launch in which direction they were searching for me. I felt that they would naturally assume that I would head northeast up the coast in the direction of Sanara, whereas my destination lay southwest—the little island where I had grounded my ship. Nor was I mistaken, for presently I heard the sound of the launch receding to my left; and I knew that it was making for the open sea by way of the easterly side of the harbor's mouth. With a sigh of relief, I kept to my course; and presently rounded the headland at the west side of the harbor and turned into the open sea. The offshore breeze was no better than that which I had had in the harbor, but I continued to hug the shore because I had one last duty to perform in Amlot before I continued on my way.

I owed much to Zerka, and I could not leave without warning her of the danger which threatened her. I knew where her palace was situated on the shore of the ocean with its gardens running down to the water line. It would delay me no more than a few minutes to stop there and warn her. I felt that I could do no less. The conditions were ideal—low tide and an offshore wind.

Silently and smoothly my light craft skimmed the surface of the water, the faint luminosity of the Amtorian night revealing the shore line as a black mass dotted with occasional lights that shone from the windows of the palaces of the rich and powerful. Even in the semi-darkness, I had no difficulty in locating Zerka's palace. I ran in as close as I could on the tack I was holding; then dropped my sail and paddled for the shore. Beaching my craft, I drew it well up toward the sea wall, where only a very high tide could have reached it; then I made my way up to the palace.

I knew that I was undergoing considerable risk, for, if Zerka were under suspicion, as I feared might be the case, she would doubtless be under surveillance. There might be watchers in the palace grounds, or even in the palace itself. For all I knew, Zerka might already be under arrest, for Narvon's dying confession was not cut off quickly enough to hide from me the identity of the accomplice he had almost named. Of course, I had already been suspicious of the truth. I did not think that the Zanis were, and so there was a possibility that they had not connected Zerka's name with that which the dying man had almost spoken. In any event, I must take this chance.

I went directly to the great doors that opened onto the terrace overlooking the gardens and the sea. On Amtor there are no doorbells, nor do people knock on doors—they whistle. Each individual has his own distinctive notes, sometimes simple, sometimes elaborate. At entrance doorways there are speaking tubes into which one whistles, and it was with some perturbation that I now whistled into the mouthpiece of the tube at the great doors of the toganja's palace.

I waited for several minutes. I heard no sound within the building. The silence was ominous. I was, nevertheless, about to repeat my whistle when the door swung partly open, and Zerka stepped out onto the terrace. Without a word, she took my hand and hurried me down into the garden where trees and shrubbery cast black shadows. There was a bench there, and she drew me down on it.

"Are you mad?" she whispered. "They were just here looking for you. The doors on the avenue had scarcely closed behind them when I heard your whistle. How did you get here?

If you can get away again, you must leave at once. There are probably spies among my servants. Oh, why did you come?"

"I came to warn you."

"Warn me? Of what?"

"I saw Narvon tortured," I said.

I felt her stiffen. "And?"

"Mephis was trying to wring the names of his accomplices from him."

"Did—did he speak?" she asked breathlessly.

"He said, 'The Toganja'; and died with the beginning of her name on his lips. I do not know that Mephis suspected, for he had not seen what I had in the house of Narvon; but I feared that he might suspect, and so I came here to take you to Sanara with me."

She pressed my hand. "You are a good friend," she said. "I knew that you would be, and it was first proved to me when you prevented that kardogan from searching the back room of Narvon's house; now you have proved it again. Yes, you are a very good friend, Carson of Venus."

That name on her lips startled me. "How did you know?" I asked. "When did you find out?"

"The morning after we dined together that first time in the evening of the day that you entered Amlot."

"But how?" I insisted.

She laughed softly. "We are all suspicious here in Amlot, suspicious of everyone. We are always searching for new friends, expecting new enemies. The instant that I saw you in that restaurant I knew that you were not of Amlot, probably not of Korva; but if you were of Korva, the chances were excellent that you were a spy from Sanara. I had to find out. Oh, how many times I have laughed when I recalled your stories of Vodaro. Why, you didn't know the first thing about that country."

"But how did you find out about me?" I demanded.

"I sent an emissary to your room in the travellers' house to search your belongings while you slept. He brought me Muso's message to Spehon."

"Oh, so that is why that was never used against me," I exclaimed. "It has had me worried ever since it disappeared, as you may well imagine."

"I wanted to tell you, but I couldn't. You have no idea how careful we have to be."

"You were very careless in going to the house of Narvon," I said.

"We hadn't the slightest reason to believe that Narvon was suspected. Now that I know how loyal you are, I don't mind telling you that we are planning a counterrevolution that will overthrow the Zanis and restore Kord to the throne."

"That can never be done," I said.

"Why?" she demanded.

"Kord is dead."

She was horrified. "You are sure?" she asked.

"I saw Mephis assassinate him." I told her the story briefly.

She shook her head sadly. "There is so much less to fight for now," she said. "Muso might easily be as bad as Mephis."

"Muso is a traitor to his own country," I said. "That message I brought you proves it clearly. I wish that I had it now to take back to Sanara with me. The army would rise against him; and with Kord dead, the people would rally around the man they love and make him jong."

"Who is that?" she asked.

"Taman," I said.

"Taman! But Taman is dead."

"Taman dead? How do you know?" My heart sank at the thought. Duare and I would have no powerful friend in Sanara.

"We heard some time ago from a captured Sanaran officer that Muso had sent him to Amlot on a dangerous mission and that he had never returned to Sanara. It was a foregone conclusion that he must be dead."

I breathed a sigh of relief. "He was returned safely to Sanara before I left there; and unless he has been killed since I came to Amlot, he is still alive."

"You shall have the message," she said. "I kept it. But how do you expect to escape from Amlot and get back through the Zani lines in safety?"

"Do you forget that Carson of Venus is the *mistal* that flies over Zani troops and drops bombs on them?" I asked.

"But the thing you fly in? You haven't that here?"

"It is not far away. I am praying that nothing has happened to it. That was the chance I had to take."

"You are so lucky that I am sure you will find it just as you left it. And, speaking of luck, how in the world did you ever get out of the city, with the entire Zani Guard looking for you? They are absolutely turning the city inside out, I am told."

"I was stopped by a detachment of the Guard on my way to the quay. Fortunately for me, it was commanded by Mantar. He is a good friend, thanks to you."

"He is one of us," she said.

"I suspected you both almost from the first, notwithstanding your Maltu Mephises and your Zani salutes."

"I was so sure of you that I was a little freer than usual. Somehow, I knew you were all right—you just couldn't have been a Zani at heart."

"We shouldn't be sitting here talking," I told her. "Go get Muso's message and a few of your belongings, and we'll be on our way to Sanara."

She shook her head. "I wish that I might," she said, "but I have a duty to perform before I leave Amlot."

"There is nothing more important than saving your life," I insisted.

"There is something more important to me than my life," she replied. "I am going to tell you what it is and why I must stay and what I am going to do—something that I have shared with only Mantar before. Mantar and my man were the closest of friends. They were officers in the same regiment of The Jong's Guard. When Mephis formed the Zani Party during the last disastrous war, my man was one of his bitterest foes. It was in the last battle of the war that my man was supposed to have been killed. His body was never found. But he was not killed in battle. A private soldier, who had been closely attached to Mantar, saw my man die; and he told Mantar the story of his end. He was tortured and murdered by a band of Zanis under direction of Mephis. When I learned this, I swore to kill Mephis; but I wished to wait until my act would be of service to my country. We are preparing for a sudden stroke at Zani power. When our forces are ready, the violent death of Mephis would throw the Zanis into at least temporary demoralization. I must be here to see that he dies a violent death at the proper time."

96

"But suppose you are suspected now and arrested? You can't carry out your plan then."

"If I am arrested, I shall still carry out my plan to kill Mephis," she said. "I shall certainly be taken before him for questioning and probably for torture; then I shall kill him. You must go now. I'll fetch Muso's message. Just a moment," and she was gone.

I felt a wave of melancholy surge through me as I sat there waiting for her to return. I knew that I should never see her again, for she was going to certain death, even if she succeeded in destroying Mephis. She was so beautiful and fine, such a loyal friend—it was tragic that she must die.

Presently she came back with Muso's message. "Here it is," she said. "I hope it puts Taman on the throne. I wish that I were to live to see that day."

Then she, too, knew that she would not! I think I loathed Mephis more that instant than I ever had before—which is saying something which no superlative can express.

"I am coming back, Zerka," I said. "Perhaps I can aid you in the overthrow of the Zanis. A few bombs at the psychological moment might help your cause. Or maybe you will have changed your mind and decided to come away with me. Now listen carefully. Southwest of Amlot is a flat-topped mountain."

"Yes," she said, "it is called Borsan."

"Two rivers join just this side of it, and in the fork of the rivers there is a farm. It belongs to a man named Lodas."

"I know him well," she said. "He is one of us—a loyal soul."

"When I come back I shall circle over the farm of Lodas," I explained. "If I see a smoke-fire lighted in one of his fields, I shall know that I am to land for a message from you—or, better still, for you, I hope. If I see no smoke, I shall fly on to Amlot and circle the city. That will throw the city into a turmoil, I am sure. You will hear of it and see me. If you are alive, you will make one smoke-fire on your beach, here. If you would like to have me bomb the palace and the barracks, you will light two smoke-fires. If I see no smoke-fire, I shall know that you are dead; and then I shall bomb hell out of the Zanis."

"What is *hell?*" she asked.

"That is something peculiar to Earthmen," I laughed. "And now I must be going. Goodby, Zerka." I touched her hand with my lips.

"Goodby, Carson of Venus," she said. "I hope that you do come back and bomb hell out of the Zanis."

XIII: DANGER IN SANARA

As I put out to sea from the beach in front of the palace of the Toganja Zerka, my mind was filled with such emotions as beggar description. My beloved Duare was in grave danger in Sanara—the greatest danger being that she might be forced to die by her own hand, which I knew she would do rather than mate with Muso. And in Amlot I was leaving behind a good friend who was in equal danger, and in the Prison of Death lay Duare's father. If ever a man's mind was beset by apprehension of dire import, it was mine that night.

Standing out from shore, I caught a brisker breeze, which finally veered into the northeast and drove me along at a spanking pace. As the wind rose, so did the seas, until I began to have doubts as to the ability of my frail craft to weather them. It was an almost following wind, and constantly I was expecting to be engulfed by the growing seas that pursued me. The lightness of my boat, however, kept me just out of danger from that cause; but there was always the possibility of striking a submerged rock or a reef in this sea of which I knew nothing. I was compelled to stay always too close to land for safety, lest I pass my little island without recognizing it as such; but at last I saw it; and, without a great deal of difficulty, made the little cove where I had previously been taken off by Lodas.

The fear that now assailed me was as to the safety of my ship. Would I find it where I had left it? What if some prowling fishermen had discovered it? I thought of a dozen reasons why it should be missing or destroyed as I drew my canoe safely out of the water and hastened across the island toward the spot where I had fastened the anotar down. At last I saw it dimly through the night, and then I was beside it. The reaction and the relief left me weak for a moment, as I realized that the ship was just as I had left it.

Casting off the ropes and throwing them into the rear cockpit, I taxied out into open meadow that formed the greater part of the island. A moment later I was in the air and heading straight for Sanara. I saw lights in Lodas's cottage as I sped past, and a moment later the lights of Amlot shone on my right. After that I saw no sign of life until the campfires of the Zani army flickered below me; and then, ahead, I could see the glow of the lights of Sanara. My Duare was there! In a few minutes I should be holding her in my arms again. I tried to open the throttle wider, only to find that it was open as far as it would go—I had been running the engine at maximum all the way from Amlot without realizing it; but I had made good time. I had left the Zani barracks and started for the quay about the 20th hour, it was now approaching only the 26th hour. In six Amtorian hours, which are equivalent to four Earth hours, I had made my escape from Amlot, sailed about ten miles along the coast, and flown to Sanara. That little gale had helped me on my way, and my light craft had practically flown the distance.

I approached Sanara without lights and at a high altitude; then I spiralled down from directly above the landing field that I had previously used. I knew every bump and depression in it, so many times had I used it. With my noiseless motor, I came in as quietly as a falling leaf; and taxied to the hangar that Muso had had built for me. The field was deserted; and the hour being late and few people on the streets in this district, I believe that no one saw my ship or saw me land. That was as I wished it, for I wanted to see Duare and Taman before I talked with anyone else.

I kept my flying helmet on to hide my Zani haircut, hoped that no one would notice my Zani trappings, and set out on foot in the direction of Taman's palace. As I approached it, I saw Muso's palace across the avenue brilliant with a thousand lights. Many gorgeously trapped gantors were waiting patiently along both sides of the avenue. Strains of music floated out into the night from the interior of the palace. I could also hear the murmur of many voices. It was evident that Muso was entertaining.

One of the sentries in front of Taman's palace stepped up to me as I stopped at the entrance.

"What do *you* want?" he demanded. I guess putting a man in front of a door anywhere in the universe must do something to him. The tremendous responsibility implicit in such a cosmic assignment seems to remove all responsibility for good manners. I have seldom known it to fail. When it does, they must immediately transfer the man to some other form of activity.

"I want to go in," I said; "I am Carson of Venus."

The fellow stepped back as though he had seen a ghost, as I imagine that he thought he had, for a moment.

"Carson of Venus!" he exclaimed. "We thought you were dead. Muso issued a proclamation of mourning for you. You must be dead."

"I am not, and I want to go in and see my wife and Taman."

"They are not there," he said.

"Where are they?"

"Across the street." He looked a bit uncomfortable as he said it, or was it my imagination?

"Then I'll go over there," I said.

"I do not think Muso will be glad to see you," opined the sentry; but I had already started, and he did not attempt to detain me.

Once again, at Muso's palace, I was stopped by a sentry. He wouldn't believe that I was Carson of Venus, and was going to have me carted off to jail. But I finally prevailed on him, by means of a small bribe, to call an officer. He who came, I had known quite well and had liked. I had taken him up in my ship a number of times, and we were good friends. When he recognized me, he looked mighty uncomfortable. I laid a hand on his arm, reassuringly.

"Please don't be embarrassed," I begged. "I have heard. Am I in time?"

"Thank the good fates, you are," he replied. "It was to be announced at the 27th hour this night. It is almost that now."

"And I may go in?" I asked, out of courtesy; for I intended going in, if I had to kill someone doing it.

"I would be the last man to stop you," he said, "even if I lost my head for it."

"Thanks," I said, and ran up the broad stairway beyond the ornate portals.

I could see down the center corridor to the great throne-room. It was packed with the aristocracy of Sanara. I knew that whatever of interest was taking place in the palace was taking place there; so I hurried along the corridor toward the doorway. Over the heads of the assembly I could see Muso standing on a dais beside the throne. He was speaking.

"A jong," he was saying, "must take his woman before the eyes of all men; so that all may know whom to honor as their vadjong. Being without a woman, I have chosen to honor one whose man gave his life in the service of Korva and myself. It is the highest award of merit that I can confer upon his memory."

I was elbowing my way through the crowd to the discomfiture of ribs and toes and to the accompaniment of scowls and muttered imprecations. Finally an officer seized me by the shoulder and swung me around facing him. When he saw who I was, his eyes went wide; and then a wry smile twisted his lips as he let me go and gave me a push forward. As I came in full view of the dais, I saw Duare sitting on a low bench, her eyes staring straight ahead, that noble little head of hers unbowed. A strapping warrior of the jong's guard sat on either side of her. That was the only reason she was there.

"And now," said Muso, "lives there any man who says I may not take Duare, Janjong of Vepaja, to be my queen?"

"There does," I said in a loud voice, stepping forward. Duare looked quickly down at me; then, before the warriors could prevent, she had leaped to the floor and flung herself into my arms.

Muso stood there with his mouth open, his arms hanging limply at his side. If the saying about having the starch taken out of one was ever appropriate, it was then. Here was a

100

situation with which it seemed impossible for him to cope. Here was a problem without a solution. Finally he forced a sickly smile.

"I thought you were dead," he said. "This is indeed a happy moment."

I just looked at him, and made no reply. The silence in the room was deathlike. It must have lasted for a full minute, which is a very long time under such circumstances; then someone started for the doorway, and like a funeral procession the guests passed out. I felt a hand on my arm, and turned to see whose it was. It was Taman's. Jahara was at his side. She looked both frightened and pleased.

"Come," he said, "you had better get out of here."

As we reached the doorway, I turned and looked back. Muso was still standing there beside his throne like one in a trance. We left the jong's palace and crossed directly to Taman's, nor did any of us breathe freely until we were seated in Jahara's boudoir.

"You will have to leave Sanara at once," said Taman—"tonight, if possible."

"I don't want to leave Sanara," I said. "At last Duare and I have found a place where we might live in peace and happiness. I shall not let one man drive me out."

"But you cannot fight the jong," he said; "and until Kord is restored, Muso is jong."

"I think I can," I said, "and I think I can create a new jong. Kord is dead."

"Kord dead? How do you know?"

"I saw Mephis kill him," and then I told them the story of the assassination of the Jong of Korva.

"And the new jong?" asked Jahara. "Who is he to be?"

"Taman," I said.

Taman shook his head. "That cannot be. I owe allegiance to Muso, if Kord be dead."

"Even if he were proved to be a traitor to his people?" I asked.

"No, not in that event, of course; but Muso is no traitor to the people of Korva."

"How many high officers of the army and officials of the government would feel as you do?" I asked.

"All but a few who owe everything to Muso," he replied.

"How many of them can you gather here tonight," I asked.

"Twenty to thirty of the most important," he said.

"Will you do it? I ask you to trust me. It will be for the best good of Korva—the country that I would wish to make my own."

He summoned several aides and gave instructions; then Taman, Jahara, and Duare settled down to listen to the story of my adventures in Amlot while we awaited the coming of the invited guests. I did not tell Duare that I had found her father a prisoner in a Zani prison until after we were alone together the next morning after the guests had left. She was very brave about it, and was confident that I would rescue him eventually.

At last the great men commenced to arrive. There were generals and councilors of state and great nobles of the realm, the flower of Korvan aristocracy that had escaped the Zani massacres. We met in the large audience chamber and were seated at a great table that had been brought into the room for the occasion. Taman was seated at the head of the table; I, being without nobility or rank, sat at the lower end. When all were seated, Taman rose.

"You all know Carson of Venus and what he has done for Sanara," he said. "He has asked me to call you together at this late hour because a national emergency exists. I trust him, and have taken his word that such is the case. I feel that we should listen to him. Are you all agreed?"

Thirty heads nodded gravely; then Taman turned to me. "You may speak, Carson of Venus," he said; "but you must have proof of what you have insinuated to me, for though you are my friend, my first duty is to my jong. Do not forget that. Proceed."

"Let me put a hypothetical question to you gentlemen before I lay my information before you," I commenced. "If it were proved beyond doubt that your jong had sought to conspire with the enemy to cause the defeat of the forces holding Sanara and turn the city over to the Zanis at a price, would you feel that you were relieved of your oaths of allegiance to him and be warranted in replacing him with one of royal blood in whom you had the utmost confidence?"

Many a face was clouded by a resentful scowl. "You are suggesting a grievous charge," said a great general.

"I am asking you a hypothetical question," I replied. "I have made no charge. Do you care to answer?"

"There is no question as to what I should do," said the general, "if such an emergency confronted me. I should be the first to turn against any jong who did such a traitorous thing as that, but that is something that no jong of Korva would do."

"And you other gentlemen?" I asked.

Without exception they all concurred in the sentiments of the general.

"Then I may tell you that such an emergency exists," I said. "I shall shock you by my disclosures, but I must have your assurance that you will hear me through and consider impartially the evidence I have to offer."

"I can assure you that we shall," said Taman.

"Muso, swearing me to secrecy, sent me to Amlot with a message for Spehon, Mephis's chief lieutenant. He chose me for two reasons. One was that he thought I could not read Amtorian, and therefore could not know what was in the message; and the other you had proof of in his palace this night—he wanted my woman. But I can read Amtorian; and after I got to Amlot, I became suspicious and read Muso's message to Spehon. In it he offered to open the gates of Sanara to Zani troops in return for the throne of Korva, and he agreed to accept Mephis as his advisor and to reward the Zanis. He also suggested that it would be best if Carson of Venus were destroyed in Amlot."

"This is preposterous!" cried a great noble. "The man must be mad to make such charges. They are prompted by jealousy, because Muso desires his woman."

"They cannot be true," exclaimed another.

"Taman," cried a third, "I demand this man's arrest."

"You are not keeping your promise to me," I reminded them. "Is this what I am to expect of Korvan nobility? And do you think I am such a fool as to make charges of this kind without ample evidence to substantiate them? What would I have to gain? I would be signing my own death warrant. I may be doing so anyway; but I am doing it for the only country on Amtor that I can call my own, the one country in which my princess and I feel that we have a chance to live happily among friends."

"Go on," said the great general. "I apologize for my confreres."

"Where are your proofs?" asked Taman.

"Here," I said, and drew Muso's message from my pocket pouch. "Here, in his own handwriting, Muso convicts himself." I handed the envelope to Taman. He opened it and read it through carefully to himself; then he passed it to the man to his right. Thus it

103

passed around the table, each man reading it carefully. It left them silent and sober-faced. Even after the last man had read it and passed it back to Taman, they sat in silence. It was the great general who spoke first.

"I do not doubt the integrity of this man or his belief in the duplicity of Muso," he said. "It is sufficient to shake the confidence of each of us. In addition, he knows that Muso sought his life. I cannot blame him for anything he may think; I should think as he does, were I he. But he is not a Korvan by birth. There is not bred in him the reverence and loyalty to our jongs that is part of every fiber of our beings. For him, this document is sufficient proof. As I have said, it would be for me, were I he; but I am not. I am a Korvan noble, the first general of the jong's armies; and so I must give Muso the benefit of every doubt. Perhaps this message was a ruse to lure the Zani troops from some part of the line, that Muso might order an attack upon that weakened part. It would have been excellent strategy. Now I suggest that we prove conclusively whether such was his intent, or whether he did intend to open the gates to the enemy."

"How may that be done?" asked Taman.

"We shall try to arrange to have the enemy shoot three blue rockets into the air before the main gates of Sanara on three successive nights; then wait and see what Muso does."

"But how can we get the enemy to co-operate?" asked another.

"I shall commission Carson of Venus to drop a message behind their lines, telling them that I should like to hold a parley with them and asking them, if they are agreeable to the suggestion, to shoot the blue rockets."

"An excellent suggestion," said Taman.

"But," I objected, "seeing me returned alive, Muso may be suspicious; for he definitely asked Spehon to have me destroyed."

"Write a report," said the general, "stating that after you delivered the message you became fearful and escaped."

"That would certainly arouse Muso's suspicions," said Taman.

"I might tell him the truth," I suggested, "and that is that the very night I arrived in Amlot the message was stolen from me. The very fact that I remained there so long should convince Muso that I had no suspicion of what the note contained."

"I think your idea is the best one," said the general; "but why did you stay so long in Amlot—if you could have escaped?"

"I had several reasons," I replied. "I suspected that Mintep, Jong of Vepaja and father of my princess, was a prisoner there. I also wanted to gather what information I could for the Sanaran high command. Lastly, I had to establish myself before I could safely make an effort to escape. I became an officer in the Zani Guard and was, for a while, acting governor of The Gap kum Rov."

"And you absorbed some information?"

"Much," I replied. "I have learned that a counterrevolution is about to be launched, the proponents of which hoped to restore Kord to his throne."

"You say 'hoped'," commented a noble. "Have they now given up the idea?"

"Kord is dead," I said.

I might as well have thrown a bomb among them. They leaped to their feet almost as one man. "Kord dead?" It was the same stunned reaction that I had seen before.

"But," cried one, "we have heard that rumor often before, but it has never been substantiated."

"I saw him die," I told them; then I had to go all over that harrowing episode again.

Well, at last they prepared to go; but before they did I propounded another question. "And now, gentlemen," I said, "just who is going to protect my princess and me from Muso? If I am not mistaken, I stand a good chance of being assassinated the first time I go on the streets."

"He is right," said the general.

"He should certainly be protected, General Varo," agreed Taman.

"Well," said Varo, "I know of no safer place for them than where they are now, under the protection of the man who is next in line for the throne of Korva, after Muso."

There was a subdued cheer at that, but I was not surprised. Taman was the most popular man in Sanara. He sat for a moment with his head bowed, and then he looked up at Varo. His face showed traces of mental strain; his manner was tinged with embarrassment.

"I wish that I might agree with you in that," he said; "but, unfortunately, I cannot. As a matter of fact, I believe that my palace would be the least safe place for Carson of Venus and the Janjong of Vepaja. During the past ten days three attempts have been made upon my life—twice by poison, once by dagger."

The disclosure so shocked the assembled nobles, that, for a moment, there was deep silence; then Varo spoke.

"Were the scoundrels apprehended?" he asked. "Do you know who they were?"

"Yes," replied Taman, "but they were only the instruments of another."

"And you know whom that may be?" asked a noble.

"I can only surmise," replied Taman. "Unfortunately, my retainers killed all three before I had an opportunity to question them."

"Perhaps I had better remain here, then," I said, "as additional protection for the next jong of Korva."

"No," said Taman. "I appreciate your generosity; but I am well protected by my own people, and there are more important things for you to do."

"You may come to my palace," said Varo. "I swear no one shall take you from there, even if I have to protect you with the entire army of Sanara."

I shook my head. "Muso will unquestionably send for me," I said. "Should you refuse to give me up, his suspicions would be aroused; and our entire plan might come to nothing. I think I have a solution of the problem."

"What is it?" asked Taman.

"Let Varo prepare his message to the enemy at once. At the same time I shall write my report to Muso. Get two officers to volunteer for extra hazardous duty. I shall want them to accompany me. As soon as Varo's message is ready, Varo can order me out on special duty. I shall take my princess and the two officers with me, drop the message behind the enemy lines, and remain away until you shall have had time to determine Muso's guilt or assure yourselves of his innocence. When I return above Sanara, liberate one balloon if it is unsafe for me ever to return to Sanara; liberate two if I am to return another day for further advice; liberate three if it is safe for me to land. In the event that I cannot land in safety to myself, I shall land the two officers the night that I get the message; and I must have your assurance now that I shall be permitted to do so and take off again in safety."

"The entire plan is excellent," said Taman. "Please put it in writing; so that there shall be no misunderstanding of the signals."

"May I ask why you wish to have two of our officers accompany you?" asked Varo.

"One of them will have to go with me into Amlot while I attempt to liberate the Jong of Vepaja from the Gap kum Rov; the other will remain with my princess and the ship while I am away in Amlot."

"I shall have no difficulty in obtaining volunteers," said Varo. "Now, if we are to get you away before dawn, we must get to work."

XIV: BACK TO AMLOT

An hour before dawn we left the palace of Taman; Duare, the two officers who had volunteered to accompany us, and I. Because of Duare, I felt nervous and uneasy; for we had to leave the palace in full view of the guards before the palace of Muso, directly across the avenue; and while the fact that Varo had furnished us with a strong guard imparted a feeling of greater security, yet, at the same time, it certainly made us extremely conspicuous. There were ten military gantors loaded with soldiers, constituting what, to me, had taken on the proportions of a pageant; and I can tell you that I breathed a sigh of relief when I had my party aboard the ship and was taxiing out for the take-off; and as we soared above the walls of Sanara and out across open country, I was happier than I had been for many days. Once again I was free, and I had Duare with me.

I had put Ulan and Legan, the two officers, in the cabin. Duare sat beside me, and there was a basket of small bombs in each cockpit. The ship was more heavily laden than it had ever before been, but that had seemed to make no appreciable difference in the take-off, nor could I see that she handled differently in flight. We had determined in Havatoo, while designing her, that she would easily lift a load of fifteen hundred pounds; so I had had little doubt that she would have no trouble with the approximately thousand-pound load that she was now carrying.

I flew slowly toward the enemy camp, killing time until daylight should have come. Ulan and Legan were thrilled beyond words, for this was the first flight either of them had taken; while Duare and I were just content to be together again, holding hands like a couple of kids.

I had hurriedly contrived a tiny parachute before leaving Taman's palace. It consisted of a square of very light fabric woven from the web of a small cousin of the targo, a giant spider that inhabits the mile-high trees that grow in many parts of Amtor; and which is so sheer as to be almost invisible, yet quite strong. To the four corners of this square piece I had tied strings, and to the ends of these strings I had attached the leather envelope which bore Varo's message to the enemy.

Dawn was just breaking as we flew over the Zani camp. An alert sentry must have sighted us, for I distinctly heard a shout; and almost immediately saw men running from the shelters which lined the streets of the camp. I continued to circle above them, well out of range of r-rays, until it was entirely light; then, estimating the velocity of the wind, I flew a little way beyond the windward side of the camp and tossed the message overboard. The little parachute opened immediately and floated gracefully down toward the camp. I could see thousands of men by now standing with upturned faces, watching it. They must have thought that it was some new engine of destruction, for when it came close to the ground near the center of the camp, they scattered like sheep. I continued to circle until I saw a brave soul advance to where the message lay and pick it up. Then I dipped a wing and flew away.

The trip to the island was uneventful. I circled Lodas's house for quite some time, but no smoke signal was lighted; then I dropped over to the island and landed. The country, except in the vicinity of the cities, is strangely deserted in every part of Amtor that I have visited. Between Sanara and the farm of Lodas we had not seen a sign of human life except that in the camp of the Zanis, which, of course, was no permanent habitation. Few farmers have the temerity that Lodas displayed in locating a farm so far from civilization, and open constantly to the danger of attack by some of the fearsome creatures which roam the plains and forests of Venus. It was, however, the very fact that few men traversed these interurban wildernesses that had rendered my little island so safe a place to hide the anotar and also the little craft that had brought me there from Amlot and which I hoped would bear me back to the Zani stronghold.

As we came in to land, I saw my boat lying where I had dragged it; and one more cause of anxiety was removed. Now I had only to wait for darkness and the proper moment to launch my attempt to rescue Mintep. I told Legan that he was to remain with Duare in the unlikely event that she should need protection, and I also instructed her to take to the air if any danger threatened them. Duare was by now an efficient pilot. I had taken her with me on many of my flights over the enemy lines, and had had her practice landings and take-offs on the surface of a dry lake I had discovered some fifty miles west of Sanara. I had also let her take off and land at the racing field in Sanara. She was quite competent to land anywhere that conditions were reasonably favorable. I drew a rough map of Amlot for her, marking the location of the palace and the barracks; and told her that if I had not returned to the island by dawn she and Legan were to fly along the coast toward Amlot, keeping a close lookout for my boat; and if they did not see me, they were to fly over the city and drop bombs on the palace and the barracks until they saw me put out into the harbor. I was sure they would be able to identify me from the air because of my flying helmet.

It had taken me about three Amtorian hours to sail from Amlot to the island. Allowing eight hours for the round trip, including the time it might take to get into the Gap kum Rov and take Mintep out, I estimated that I should leave the Island about the 29th hour in order to get back by dawn. In the event that Ulan and I never returned, Duare was to take Legan back to Sanara; and if three balloons were sent up, indicating that it was safe to land, she should do so; for I felt that she would be safer there than anywhere else. If the signal were a discouraging one, she might try to reach Vepaja; but that would be almost suicidal, since she could not approach anywhere near Kooaad, her city, in the ship; and the dangers she would encounter on the ground were far too numerous and terrible to render it at all likely that she would survive.

"Do not even think of anything so terrible as that you may not return from Amlot," she begged. "If you do not, it will make no difference where I go, for I shall not live. I do not care to live unless I have you, Carson."

Ulan and Legan were on the ground inspecting the boat; so I took her in my arms and kissed her, and told her that I would come back.

"For no one but your father would I go to Amlot and risk your life as well as my own," I said.

"I wish you did not have to go, Carson. What a strange retribution it would be if, for the sake of the throne I gave up for you, I should lose you. It would not be just retribution, though—it would be wicked."

"You'll not lose me, dear," I assured her, "unless your father takes you away from me."

"He can't do that now. Even though he is my father and my jong, I should disobey him if he sought to."

"I'm afraid he's going to be—well, disagreeable about the matter," I suggested. "You know how shocked you were at the very thought of even talking to me. When I told you I loved you, you wanted to knife me; and you really felt that I deserved death. How do you suppose he's going to feel about it when he finds that you are irrevocably mine? He'll want to kill me."

"When are you going to tell him?" she asked.

"After I get him here on the island. I'm afraid he'd upset the boat if I told him at sea."

She shook her head dubiously. "I don't know," she said—"I can't imagine how he'll take it. He is a very proud jong, steeped in the traditions of a royal family that extends back into prehistoric times; and, Carson, he does not know you as I do. If he did, he would be glad that his daughter belonged to such as you. Do you know, Carson, he may even kill me. Even though you think you know, yet you have no conception of the taboos and interdictions that dictate the attitude of all toward the sacred person of the virgin daughter of a jong. There is nothing in your life with which I may compare it. There is nothing that you so reverence and hold so sacred."

"Yes, there is, Duare," I said.

"What?" she demanded.

"You."

"Fool!" she said, laughing. "But you're a dear fool, and I know that you believe what you said."

The day drew to a close and the night wore on. Ulan and Legan amused themselves by fishing; and we built a fire and cooked what they caught, enjoying an unexpectedly excellent meal. I cut a slender sapling about twenty feet long and stowed it in the boat. As the 29th hour approached, I kissed Duare goodby. She clung to me for a long time. I know she thought it was the last time she should ever see me. Then Ulan and I embarked. A good breeze was blowing; and we skimmed away into the darkness, bound for Amlot.

Did you ever reach into an inside pocket time after time to assure and reassure yourself that you had not forgotten the theater tickets that you knew were there? Well, that's the way I kept feeling in my pocket pouch for the duplicate master key to the cells of The Prison of Death I had had made just before I left Amlot. And not without reason was I thus solicitous—without that key, not even an act of God could have gotten Mintep's cell door unlocked without the co-operation of Torko; and somehow I couldn't see Torko co-operating.

We rounded the headland and drew into the harbor of Amlot just before the 3rd hour. Running before the wind, we approached the little island of horror where loomed the Gap kum Rov. As we came closer to shore I lowered the sail, lest its white expanse be seen by some watchful Zani eye, and paddled quietly in beneath those frowning walls. Feeling my way cautiously along the cold, damp stones, I came at last to that which I sought—the opening of the chute through which the ashes of burned men are discharged into the bay. Ulan and I spoke no word, as all the way from the island I had been coaching him on what he was to do; so that it would be unnecessary for us to speak in other than an emergency. Once more I felt to learn if I still had the key; then, as Ulan held the boat in position beneath the mouth of the chute, I carefully inserted the pole I had prepared and pushed it up its full length, letting the lower end rest on the bottom of the boat. This done, I proceeded to climb up the pole into the chute. Disturbed by the pole and my body brushing the sides of the chute, the ashes of a thousand dead men drifted gently down upon me.

When I reached the top of the pole, I raised one hand directly over my head. To my vast relief, it came in contact with the trap door just a few inches above me. I pushed up, and raised it far enough so that I could grasp the sill with my fingers; then remained quiet, listening. Only the moans and groans of the prisoners came to my ears. There was no alarm. So far, none had heard me. Pulling myself up, I raised the door with my head and shoulders until I could fall forward with the upper half of my body on the floor of the furnace room. A moment later I stood erect.

A few steps brought me to the dimly lighted corridor. I knew exactly where Mintep's cell lay, and walked directly to it. Whatever I was to do must be done quickly and silently. Pressing my face to the bars, I looked in. I thought I saw a figure in the far corner, a figure huddled on the floor. I inserted the key in the lock and turned it. The door swung in. I crossed and kneeled beside the figure, listening. By the breathing, I knew that the man slept. I shook him lightly by the shoulder, and as he stirred I cautioned him to silence.

"Are you Mintep?" I asked, fearful that he might have been taken to his death and another placed in his cell since I had located it. I had not served in this prison without having learned how quickly changes might come, how unexpectedly one man might be rubbed out to make place for another. I held my breath waiting for his reply. At last he spoke.

"Who are you?" he demanded.

"Never mind that," I snapped a little irritably. "Are you Mintep?"

"Yes," he said.

"Come with me quietly. Duare is waiting for you."

That was enough. Like a new man, he came to his feet and followed me stealthily to the furnace room, though I could see that he staggered a little from weakness. It was no small job getting him down that pole. He was too weak to climb down himself; so I had practically to carry him. But at last we were in the boat. I lowered the pole into the water and pushed off. We paddled all the way to the mouth of the harbor, as otherwise we would have had to tack back and forth several times to have made it; and I was afraid the sail might attract attention from the shore. Had it, a launch must certainly have overhauled us before we could get out into the open sea. But at last we turned the headland, and Ulan hoisted the sail.

Then it was that I thought to do a very foolish thing. Once I had stopped and seen Zerka while I was escaping from Amlot. It had seemed very simple and quite safe. Conditions of tide and wind were again favorable. Why not do it again? I might obtain information that would be of value to my friends at Sanara. I told Ulan and Mintep what I intended doing. It was not for them to question my judgment; so they concurred. It was the first time that we had dared speak, so fearful had we been of discovery, knowing, as we did, how the sound of voices carries over water.

"Who are you?" asked Mintep.

"Do you recall the prison officer who sang a song to you?" I asked.

"But he was a Zani," said Mintep.

"Only posing as a Zani to find you," I told him.

"But who are you?" he insisted.

"For some time I was a guest-prisoner in your palace at Kooaad," I said. "I am the stranger called Carson."

"Carson!" he exclaimed. "When Kamlot returned to Kooaad, he told me of all that you had done to serve my daughter, Duare. And now you say she is safe and waiting for me?"

"Yes; in two or three hours you shall see her."

"And you have done all this for me?" he asked.

"For Duare," I said, simply.

He made no comment on the correction, and we sailed on in silence again until we came opposite the palace of Zerka; then I turned the boat's nose in toward shore. Alas, what stupid things one does! The palace was lighted much as I had last seen it—all seemed quiet and peaceful. I hoped Zerka would be alone. I wanted only a few swift words with her.

"Stay in the boat," I told Ulan, "and be ready to push off on an instant's notice;" then I walked up the garden to the great doors that open onto the terrace. I paused and listened, but I could hear nothing; then I whistled—and waited. I did not have to wait long. I heard the sound of men running, but the sounds did not come from the house—they came from the garden behind me. I wheeled, and in the light from the palace windows I saw a dozen Zani Guardsmen running toward me.

"Shove off, Ulan!" I cried at the top of my voice. "Shove off, and take Mintep to Duare! I command it!" Then they were upon me.

At the sound of my voice the great doors swung open, and I saw more Zani uniforms in the great hall of the palace of the Toganja Zerka. They dragged me in, and when I was recognized a sullen murmur filled the room.

XV: Tragic Error

There is nothing more annoying than to commit an egregious error of judgment and have no one but yourself upon whom to blame it. As I was dragged into that room, I was annoyed. I was more than annoyed—I was frightened; for I saw certain death staring me in the face. And not death alone—for I remembered Narvon. I wondered if I would go to pieces, too.

And there was some reason for my apprehension, for besides a company of Zani Guardsmen and officers, there were a number of the great men of Zanism—there were even Mephis and Spehon themselves. And to one side, their wrists manacled, stood Zerka and Mantar. There was an expression almost of anguish in Zerka's eyes as they met mine. Mantar shook his head sadly, as though to say, "You poor fool, why did you stick your head into the noose again?"

"So you came back!" rasped Mephis. "Don't you think that was a little unwise, a little stupid?"

"Let us say unfortunate, Mephis," I replied. "Unfortunate for you."

"Why unfortunate for me?" he demanded, almost angrily. I could see that he was nervous. I knew that he was always fearful.

"Unfortunate, because you would like to kill me; but if you do—if you harm me in any way or harm the Toganja Zerka or Mantar—you shall die shortly after dawn."

"You dare threaten *me*?" he roared. "You stinking mistal! You dare threaten the great Mephis? Off to the Gap kum Rov with him!—with all of them! Let Torko do his worst with them. I want to see them writhe. I want to hear them scream."

"Wait a minute, Mephis," I advised him. "I wasn't threatening you. I was merely stating facts. I know what I'm talking about, for I have given orders that I know will be carried out if I am not safely out of Amlot shortly after dawn."

"You lie!" he almost screamed.

I shrugged. "If I were you, though, I'd give instructions that none of us is to be tortured or harmed in any way until at least the third hour tomorrow—and be sure to have a boat ready that I and my friends can sail away in after you have released us."

"I shall never release you," he said; but nevertheless he gave instructions that we were not to be tortured or harmed until he gave further orders.

And so Zerka and Mantar and I were dragged away to the Gap kum Rov. They didn't abuse us, and they even took the manacles off Zerka and Mantar. They put us all together in a cell on the second floor, which surprised me; as the basement was reserved for Mephis's special hates as well as prisoners concerning whose incarceration he would rather not have too much known.

"Why did you do such a foolish thing as to come back?" asked Zerka, after we had been left alone.

"And right after I risked my life to get you out of here," said Mantar, laughingly.

"Well," I explained, "I wanted to see Zerka and find out if there is any way in which the loyal forces at Sanara may co-operate with you."

"They could," she said, "but now they'll never know. We need more weapons—you might have brought them in that flying boat you have told me about."

"I may yet," I assured her.

"Have you gone crazy?" she demanded. "Don't you know, regardless of that courageous bluff you tried to pull, that we are all lost—that we shall be tortured and killed, probably today."

"No," I said. "I know we may, but not that we shall. I was pulling no bluff. I meant what I said. But tell me, what caused them to arrest you and Mantar?"

"It was the culmination of growing suspicion on the part of Spehon," explained Zerka. "My friendship for you had something to do with it; and after Horjan informed on you and you escaped from the city, Spehon, in checking over all your connections, recalled this friendship and also the fact that Mantar and you were close friends and that Mantar was my friend. One of the soldiers in the detail that Mantar commanded the evening that he met you and let you proceed to the quay reported to Spehon that he thought your description, which he heard after he returned to the barracks, fitted the man with whom Mantar had talked. Then, these things having suggested my connection with you, Spehon recalled Narvon's last words—the same words that assured you that I was one of those who conspired with Narvon against the Zanis. So, all in all, they had a much clearer case against me than the Zanis ordinarily require; but Mephis would not believe that I had conspired against him. He is such an egotistical fool that he thought that my affection for him assured my loyalty."

"I was, until recently, in a quandary as to your exact sentiments and your loyalties," I said. "I was told that you were high in the esteem of Mephis, that you were the author of the 'Maltu Mephis!' gesture of adulation, that it was you who suggested having citizens stand on their heads while they cheered Mephis, that it was your idea to have *The Life of Our*

115

Beloved Mephis run continuously in all theaters, and to have Zani Guardsmen annoy and assault citizens continually."

Zerka laughed. "You were correctly informed," she said. "I was the instigator of those and other schemes for making Zanism obnoxious and ridiculous in the eyes of the citizens of Amlot; so that it might be easier to recruit members for our counterrevolution. So stupidly egotistical are the chief Zanis, they will swallow almost any form of flattery, however ridiculous and insincere it may be."

While we were talking, Torko came stamping up the stairs to our cell. He had been absent from the prison when we were brought in. He wore one of his most fearsome frowns, but I could see he was delighted with the prospect of baiting and doubtless torturing such important prisoners as we. He stood and glowered at us a moment before he spoke. It was so evident that he was trying to impress and frighten us that I couldn't restrain a desire to laugh—well, perhaps I didn't try very hard. I knew how to bait such creatures as Torko. I also knew that no matter what attitude we assumed toward him he would give us the works, so to speak, the moment he was given the opportunity.

"What are you laughing at?" he demanded.

"I wasn't laughing before you came up, Torko; so I must be laughing at you."

"Laughing at me, are you, you stinking mistal?" he bellowed. "Well, you won't laugh when I get you in the courtroom tomorrow morning."

"You won't get me into the courtroom tomorrow morning, Torko; and even if I am there, you won't be. You'll be in one of these cells; and then, later, you'll have an opportunity to discover how effective are the ingenious devices for torture you bragged of having invented."

Zerka and Mantar looked their astonishment, the former smiling a little because she thought I was bluffing again. Torko stood there fairly boiling.

"I've a good mind to take you down there now," he threatened, "and get out of you what you mean by such talk."

"You wouldn't dare do that, Torko," I told him. "You already have your orders about us. And, anyway, you don't have to—I'll tell you without being tortured. It's like this: Mephis is going to be angry with you when I tell him you offered to give me liberties while I was stationed here if I would speak a good word about you to the Toganja Zerka, that she might carry it to him. He won't like it when he learns that you let me go fishing whenever I wanted to and thus permitted me to pave the way for my escape by boat; and, Torko, there is another thing that is going to make him so furious that—well, I just don't know what he will do to you when he discovers it."

116

Torko was commencing to look uncomfortable, but he came right through with the same argument that even great statesmen of our own Earth use when they're caught red-handed.

"They're a pack of lies!" he yelled.

"He won't think so when he learns about the other thing you have done—something that he can see with his own eyes," I baited him.

"What's the other lie," he demanded, his curiosity and fear getting the better of him.

"Oh, just that you unlocked the cell of Mintep, Jong of Vepaja, and let him escape," I said.

"That *is* a lie," he cried.

"Well, go and look for yourself," I suggested. "If he's gone, who else could have unlocked his cell? You have the only keys."

"He's not gone," he said; but he turned and ran down the stairs as fast as he could go.

"You seem to be having a good time," said Mantar, "and we might as well have all the fun we can while we may. It's not going to be so funny when morning comes—not for us."

"On the contrary," I objected, "that may be the most amusing time of all."

"I am amused now," said Zerka. "How furious Torko will be when he discovers that you have hoaxed him into running all the way down to the basement."

"But it is not a hoax," I said. "He will find Mintep's cell door open and Mintep gone."

"How can you possibly know that?" demanded Zerka.

"Because I released Mintep myself, and he is on his way to safety right now."

"But how could you enter the Gap kum Rov and take a prisoner out under the noses of the Zani Guard?" demanded Zerka. "Why, it is simply impossible. You couldn't have even unlocked his cell if you had managed to get into the prison, which, in itself, would have been impossible."

I had to smile. "But I did," I said, "and it was very easy."

"Would you mind very much telling me how you did it?" she asked.

"Not at all," I assured her. "In the first place, I secured a duplicate master key to all the locks of Gap kum Rov while I was stationed here. Last night I came in a boat to the side of the prison and entered it through the chute that discharges the ashes from the furnace into the bay. I brought Mintep out the same way."

Mantar and Zerka shook their heads in astonishment. It could not have seemed possible to many inhabitants of Amlot that a prisoner might escape from the Gap kum Rov, for few of them knew anything about the prison except that no prisoner had ever escaped from it.

"And you have a master key to the locks?" asked Mantar.

I took it from my pocket pouch. "Here it is," I said. "If they had confined us in the basement, we might have escaped easily, at least as far as the waters of the bay; but with a guard watching constantly on the floor below there is no chance from here."

"But aren't you afraid they'll find the key on you?" asked Zerka.

"Yes, of course; but what can I do about it? I have no place to hide it. I shall simply have to take the chance that they won't search me—they are so stupid. Anyway, unless they confine us in the basement, it cannot possibly be of any use to us. Furthermore, I have an idea that we'll walk out of here without any need of a key."

"You are very optimistic," said Mantar; "but I can't see upon what food your optimism thrives."

"Wait for dawn," I counselled.

"Listen!" said Zerka.

From below we heard Torko's voice bellowing orders. Guards were running to and fro. They were searching the prison for Mintep. When they reached our floor they entered every cell and searched it carefully, although they could have seen the whole interior of each of them from the corridor. Torko's face was drawn and pale. He looked to me like a broken man. When he reached our cell he was trembling, as much, I think, from fright as from rage.

"What have you done with him?" he demanded.

"I?" I asked in feigned astonishment. "Now, how could I have gotten into this impregnable prison, so ably guarded by the great Torko—unless with the connivance of Torko? Mephis will be sure to ask that very question."

"Listen," Torko said, coming close and whispering. "I was good to you when you were here. Do not send me to my death. Do not tell Mephis that Mintep has escaped. If he is not told, he may never know it. The chances are he has forgotten all about Mintep by this time. If you do not tell him, I promise not to torture you and your accomplices unless I am forced to; and then I'll make it as easy as I can."

"If you do torture us, I'll certainly tell him," I replied. I certainly had Torko over a barrel.

Torko scratched his head in thought for a moment. "Say," he said at last, "of course you couldn't have let him out; but how in the world did you know he was gone?"

"I'm psychic, Torko," I told him. "I even know things are going to happen before they do. What is the hour?"

He looked at me rather fearfully as he replied. "It is the 1st hour," he said. "Why?"

"Presently you shall hear a great noise in the direction of the palace of Mephis," I said, "and then word will pass around that death and destruction are raining upon the Zanis from the sky because they hold me and my friends prisoners in Gap kum Rov. When Mephis sets us free, it shall stop."

"Rubbish!" said Torko, and went on to search other cells for Mintep, Jong of Vepaja. He didn't find him.

Time dragged leadenly after dawn crept slowly out of the east and its light sought to penetrate the dirty windows of the Gap kum Rov. I was tense from waiting for the first detonation of a bomb. The second hour came and then the third, yet still nothing had happened. What could the reason be? Had disaster overtaken Duare? I imagined a hundred terrible things that might have happened. A crack-up at the take-off seemed the most likely. I was still worrying when Torko came with a detail of the guard and took us down to the courtroom. There were Mephis, Spehon, and a number of other high Zanis. We were lined up before them. They glowered at us like ogres out of a fairy tale.

"It is the third hour," said Mephis. "I have waited, and because you have made me wait it shall go the harder for you. If any of you expect any mercy you will name all your accomplices in the low plot you have fostered to overthrow the state. Torko, take the woman first. We'll make her talk, and I'll save you for the last. Take that thing off his head, Torko." He pointed at me.

I looked at Torko, as he took off my flying helmet and threw it into a corner. The sweat was pouring down his face, although it was not hot. "Do not forget, Torko," I whispered.

"Mercy," he pleaded. "I must obey orders."

They laid Zerka upon a hideous thing that would have crushed her slowly, inch by inch, starting at her toes; and they brought a brazier containing a pot of molten metal and set it down on a table beside her. It was not difficult to guess how they intended to use it. I turned my head, for I could not look at the frightful thing they contemplated.

"Do you wish to confess?" asked Mephis.

"No," replied Zerka in a firm voice.

"Have you anything to say?" he inquired.

"Yes, this: I joined the Zani Party because I had learned that you tortured and murdered my man. I joined to undermine it; and for another, greater purpose—to kill you."

Mephis laughed. "And this is the way you kill me!" he taunted.

"No, not this way; nor the way I had hoped, but the only way I could find," replied Zerka.

"What do you mean?" demanded Mephis.

"I mean that I have avenged my husband, but you did not know it. Know it now, then. Before another day has passed, you will be dead."

"And how, please, am I to die at the hand of a dead woman?" jeered Mephis.

"You ate food in my home last night, Mephis. Do you recall? That food was poisoned. I have kept it there for a long time to cheat you of the pleasure of killing me, were I caught. Last night I had the opportunity I had never hoped for of letting you eat it instead. At any moment, now, you will die—certainly before another day has passed."

The face of Mephis turned livid. He tried to speak, but no words came to his white lips. He rose and pointed at Torko. He was trying to order the torture to proceed. Torko looked at me and trembled. The other Zanis were staring at Mephis; then, close by, came a shattering detonation that shook the walls of Gap kum Rov. Duare had come! But she was bombing the prison instead of the palace—she must have mistaken the one for the other. It was possible.

"I warned you!" I shouted. "The city will be destroyed if you don't set us free and give us a boat."

"Never!" cried Mephis. "Destroy them all!" Then he gasped, clutched his throat, and fell forward across the bench.

The Zanis rushed forward, surrounding him. Another bomb burst so close that I was certain that it had struck the building. It threw us all to the floor. Spehon was the first to his feet.

120

"Mephis is dead!" he cried. "Spehon is ruler of Korva!"

"Maltu Spehon!" shouted the assembled Zanis; then a bomb exploded in the rear of the building, and again we were all thrown to the floor.

"Get them out of here!" screamed Spehon. "Get them a boat! Hurry!"

Well, they got us out of there in short order; but we were far from safe. Bombs kept bursting all around us. In the sky above, I saw the anotar circling like a great bird of prey; yet it looked sweet to me. They hurried us to a safer part of the bay side and found us a boat—a fair size fishing boat with two sails; then they hustled us into it. We made sail quickly and started tacking for the harbor entrance; and as we moved slowly away from shore, I saw the anotar drop in a graceful spiral toward us. Duare was coming to make sure that it was I. She didn't drop far enough to be in range of any r-ray or T-ray guns they might have trained on the ship, for I had warned her against this. She circled us a few times, and then flew back over the city. I wondered why she didn't follow us out to sea and pick us up. We were about the center of the harbor when I heard another bomb explode. In rapid succession five more fell. It was then that I guessed the truth—Duare had not recognized me! She must naturally have expected to see a man alone in a boat—a man wearing a flying helmet. Instead she had seen two men and a woman, and both men sported the Zani coiffure.

Briefly I explained our situation to Zerka and Mantar. It seemed almost hopeless. We could not return to shore because the Zanis would be furious at the continued bombing which I had promised them would stop if they set us free. If we waited around in the harbor on the chance that Duare might circle above us again and give me an opportunity to signal her, it was almost certain that the Zanis would send a launch out to recapture us.

"Perhaps," I suggested, "Duare may take another look, even out at sea. Suppose we round the headland and wait out of sight of the city?"

They both agreed that it would do no harm, and so I sailed the boat well out beyond the mouth of the harbor, where we would be hidden from the city by the headland. From that position we could see the anotar circling high over Amlot, and from time to time we heard the booming detonations of her bombs. Late in the afternoon we saw her turn her nose northeast in the direction of Sanara, and in a few minutes she was out of sight.

XVI: Despair

For a few minutes I plumbed the depths of despair, and then I thought of the torture chamber and how much worse things might have been for us, especially for Zerka and Mantar. Had I not stopped at her palace the night before, both of them would now be dead. They must have been thinking this same thing, too, for they were very gay and happy. Yet our position was far from being an enviable one. We were without food, water, or weapons, in a none too substantial boat, off an enemy shore; and Sanara was five hundred miles away and possibly in the hands of another enemy. But worst of all, for me, Duare was in equal danger. She would not dare return to Sanara until she knew that Muso had been deposed. If he were never deposed, what was she to do? Where could she go? And all the time she must be thinking that I was dead. I was that much better off, at least; I was sure she lived. Of course, she had her father; but I knew that that would scarcely compensate for the loss of the man she loved, nor would her father be able to protect her as well as I. He would have been all right as a protector back in his own kingdom, with his warriors and his other loyal subjects about him, but I had learned to take care of Duare under conditions far different. Of course, I hadn't always made such a good job of it; but in the end, I had come through all right.

As the anotar disappeared in the distance I made sail again and turned up the coast in the direction of Sanara.

"Where are we going?" asked Zerka.

I told her.

She nodded in approval. "I only asked out of curiosity," she said. "Wherever you wish to go suits me. Thanks to you, we are alive. We can ask no more."

"Perhaps we are as well off anyway," I said. "It might have been pretty nearly impossible to crowd seven people into the anotar."

We sailed up the coast all that night under a fresh breeze, and in the morning I came in close and we watched for signs of fresh water. At last we saw a stream falling over a low cliff into the ocean, and I made for a strip of yellow sand where a long, low surf broke lazily.

We were all suffering from thirst, which is the only excuse I had for landing in such a spot. Fortunately the boat drew little water, and we were able to paddle it in to a point where we could wade. I held it there, while Zerka and Mantar slaked their thirst; then I went and drank my fill. We had nothing in which to carry water; so we put off again immediately, hoping we might find a more suitable spot where we might make a temporary camp and endeavor to improvise some sort of equipment. About the middle of the day, we found such a place—a little cove into which a stream of fresh water emptied, and about which grew a variety of trees and plants. Among the latter was a huge arborescent grass nearly a foot in diameter, with hard, smooth outer wood and a pithy core. We managed to break one of these down; and, after building a fire, we burned out one section. The sections were formed by well marked joints or nodes, at which the inner cavity was closed by a strong diaphragm. Our efforts resulted in a receptacle about three feet high and a foot in diameter, in which we could carry fresh water. So successful was this first attempt that we made two more of them.

In the wood we found nuts and fruits; so that now all we lacked were weapons. If we had had a knife we might have fulfilled this want, as we could have made bows, arrows, and spears from the hard, outer wood of this bamboolike plant. Mantar and I discussed this most important matter, for we knew that if we were ever compelled to remain on shore for any length of time we might need weapons sorely. We certainly should, if we were to have meat to eat. We searched the beach together, and finally found several pieces of sharp-edged stones and shells. With this meager encouragement, we decided to camp where we were until we had contrived some sort of weapons.

I shall not bore you with a recital of our methods. Suffice it to say that our technique was wholly primitive; but with fire and using our sharp-edged tools as wedges and scrapers, we managed to hack out spears, bows, arrows and sharp-pointed wooden knives. We also made two long harpoons for spearing fish; then, with a supply of fresh water and quantities of nuts and tubers, we set out again upon our long journey toward Sanara.

Fortune favored us, for the wind held; and though we had a few stiff blows, the seas were never such as we could not weather. This was fortunate for us, as we did not want to be forced ashore if we could avoid it. We often ran rather close in, and at such times it was not unusual for us to see savage beasts along the shore. No monsters of the sea attacked us. In fact, we saw but a couple that might have proved dangerous; and we left these strictly alone. With our harpoons we were able to vary our diet of nuts and tubers with excellent fish, which we ran ashore and cooked as quickly as we could find a suitable place after catching them.

Had I not had my mind filled almost entirely with thoughts of Duare and worries concerning her, I might have enjoyed this adventure exceedingly; but as it was I chafed at every delay, even to the point of begrudging the time it took to cook food or take on fresh water.

On the night of the sixth day out, we were sailing smoothly along a low coast, when I saw clearly in the night sky the flare of a blue rocket against the lower surface of the inner cloud envelope. It was followed in a moment by another and then another. The enemy were springing the trap that was to snare Muso! I wondered if this were the first, the second, or the third night. We might have been too far away before this to have seen them.

123

It made no difference, as it might be two more days before we could hope to reach the coast near Sanara.

The next night we watched for a repetition of the rockets, the purpose of which I had explained to Zerka and Mantar; but nothing rewarded our vigil; and I was of the opinion that last night's rockets had completed the series of three nightly for three nights and that tonight Muso would walk into the trap that I had prepared for him. How I wished that I might be there to witness his undoing!

And now we encountered storms. The next day we were driven ashore by a wind of almost hurricane velocity. We managed to find a sheltered bay; and here we anchored, safe from the storm as well as from wild beasts and savage men. For three days we were storm-bound, and Sanara only one day's sail away! The delay was maddening, but there was nothing that we could do about it. Man made obstacles we might overcome, but not those interposed by the elements. During our enforced wait, we speculated upon our chances of gaining entry into Sanara through the Zani lines which encircled the city; and we were all forced to admit that they seemed rather remote, as, by all means, we must avoid being recaptured by the Zanis; so here was a man made obstacle quite as difficult of negotiation as any that the elements might raise. It appeared that we were stymied. However, we must go on, hoping for some fortuitous circumstance that would solve our difficulty.

In the evening of the third day, the storm suddenly abated; and, though the seas were still running high, we put out from our little harbor and set our course once more for Sanara. Perhaps it was a foolhardy thing to do, but the enforced delay and my anxiety to reach Sanara and be re-united with Duare had rendered me temerarious. The seas were like a great, grey army rushing, battalion after battalion, in their assault upon the shore; and we a tiny Argo between the Charybdis of the one and the Scylla of the other. Yet we came through without mishap, and dawn found us off the mouth of the river upon which Sanara lies a few miles from the coast.

"And now what are we to do?" asked Zerka.

I shook my head in despair. "Pray to Lady Luck," I said.

"The only plan that I can suggest that seems to contain even a germ of success," said Mantar, "is for me to get through the Zani lines at night and seek admission to the city. I am well known to many of the nobility and high officials. They would accept and believe me; and I should be safe even though Muso were still jong, which would not hold true with you, Carson. Once inside the city, it would be easy to arrange for your princess to fly out and pick up Zerka and you."

"If she is there," I amended. "If Muso is still jong, she is not there."

"That is what I must ascertain," he replied.

124

"And what of Zerka?" I asked. "If you are in the city and Muso is jong, I cannot come in; then how shall we get Zerka in?"

"I shall be content to remain with you, Carson; so don't give me a thought," said Zerka.

"Whatever we do can't be done until after dark," I said; "so we shall have to cruise around until then. Maybe in the meantime we shall have evolved a better plan than Mantar's, which I do not like because it subjects him to too much risk."

It was very monotonous, cruising aimlessly about; and very tantalizing to be so near our goal and yet so far from reaching it. The seas had gone down, but enormous ground swells alternately lifted us to high crests and dropped us into deep hollows. Fishes swarmed about us—the sea was alive with them, and now and again some great monster of the deep passed close, like a giant submarine, as it voraciously gobbled the lesser creatures in its path. About the 8th hour Zerka voiced an exclamation of excitement and pointed toward the city; and as I looked, I saw the anotar above Sanara. It was evident that she had just risen from the city. That could mean but one thing to me; no, two—the first, that Duare lived; the second, that Muso no longer ruled as jong; for no one but Duare could fly the ship, and she would not have been in Sanara had Muso ruled the city.

As we watched, we saw that the plane was heading in our direction and we prepared to try to attract Duare's attention to us. I lowered the sails, lest it hide our efforts; and then I put one of our improvised water containers upside down over the end of the harpoon. As the ship approached, Mantar and I waved the crude signal back and forth.

From the time that she had left the city, Duare had been climbing; and had gained considerable altitude by the time she passed over us. We must have appeared very small to her. Perhaps she did not see us at all. She certainly gave no indication of it. I wondered why she was flying out over the ocean, and waited for her to circle back, hoping for better luck with our signalling next time. But she did not circle back—she continued straight upon her course into the southeast. In utter silence we watched until the ship became a little speck in the distance and finally disappeared.

My heart sank, for I knew the truth—Duare thought me dead and was flying back to Vepaja with her father! I should never see her again, for how could I reach Vepaja? and what would it avail me were I to? Mintep would have me destroyed before I could even so much as see my Duare. I was utterly unnerved as I sat there staring out across that lonely ocean after my lost love. I must have looked the picture of dejection that I felt. Zerka placed a hand upon mine. It was a gesture of sympathy and friendship which would have been negatived by words.

Presently I hoisted the sails again and headed in for shore. As we approached it, and it became evident that I was going to enter the mouth of the river, Mantar spoke.

"What are you going to do?" he asked.

"I am going through the Zani lines and up to the city," I replied.

"Have you gone mad?" he demanded. "At night you might stand a chance of getting through; but in broad daylight, none. You'll be arrested; and even if no one at the front recognizes you, there'll be plenty in Amlot, where you'll surely be sent."

"I'll get through," I said, "or I won't; but I'll not go back to Amlot."

"You're desperate now, Carson," said Zerka. "Don't throw your life away uselessly. There may be happiness for you yet; why, your princess may even return from Vepaja."

"No," I said; "once she is there they will never permit her to leave again."

I ran the boat close to the river bank and leaped ashore. "Cruise around close by," I called to Mantar. "I'll get word to you, if it's humanly possible. Watch the city. If you see balloons go up by day or rockets by night, you'll know I've won through and that plans are being made to bring you and Zerka in. Goodby!"

I had run the boat quite a distance up the river before landing; so the city was not far away as I set out on foot toward it. I made no effort to conceal myself, but walked boldly toward my goal. I should have been close behind the Zani lines, but I saw no sign of troops nor of any engines of war. Presently I came to where the Zanis had lain for so many months. The ground was littered with the rubbish of war. There were a few dead men lying where they had fallen, but no living thing was visible between me and the city. The siege had been raised, the Zanis were gone!

I turned and almost ran back to the river. Mantar and Zerka were drifting slowly down the stream toward the ocean. I shouted to them and beckoned them to return, and when they were within reach of my voice I told them that the Zanis had gone and that nothing lay between us and the city. They could scarcely believe the good news; and when they had taken me aboard, we sailed up the river toward Sanara. About a quarter of a mile from the city we came ashore and walked toward the nearest gate. From the city walls a number of warriors were watching us, and, I presume, with a great deal of suspicion, since Mantar and I still wore the Zani hairdress and apparel.

As we came closer to the gate, Mantar and I made the sign of peace; and as we stopped before it an officer hailed us.

"Ho, Zanis! What do you want at Sanara? to be shot as traitors?"

"We are not Zanis," I replied. "We want word with Taman."

"So," he laughed, "you are not Zanis! Oh, no, not at all. Do you think we of Sanara do not know Zanis when we see them?"

"I am Carson of Venus," I said. "Tell that to Taman."

At that he left the wall; and presently the gate swung open a little way, and he came out with a few warriors to have a closer look at us. As he did so, I recognized him; and he me. He was one of the officers who had flown with me on one of the occasions that I had bombed the Zani camp. I introduced him to Zerka and Mantar, for whom I vouched; and he told us to enter the city and that he would escort us personally to Taman.

"One question," I said, "before I come into Sanara."

"And what is that?" he asked.

"Is Muso still jong?"

He smiled. "I can understand that you might wish to know that," he said, "but I can assure you that Muso is no longer jong. The high council deposed him and created Taman jong."

It was with a feeling of relief that I re-entered the city of Sanara after the trying weeks of danger and uncertainty through which I had passed, and during which I had never known of any place upon this strange planet where I might abide in safety—not in Kooaad, where even my best friends would have been in duty bound to have killed me because I had dared love their princess and she me; not in Kapdor, the Thorist city of Noobol, where they had placed me in the room of the seven doors from which no man before had escaped alive; not in Kormor, Skor's city of the dead, from which I had stolen Duare and Nalte from under Skor's nose in his own palace; not in Havatoo, that Utopian city on the banks of the River of Death, from which I had rescued Duare from an inexplicable miscarriage of justice; not in Amlot, where the followers of Spehon would have torn me limb from limb. There was only Sanara. Had Muso still been jong here I should have been doomed to wander on in hopeless loneliness.

At last I had a city I might call my own, where I might establish a home and live in peace and contentment; but there was only relief, not joy, in contemplation of the fact, because Duare was not there to share it with me. So I re-entered Sanara in sorrow, and in the howdah of a great military gantor we were escorted through the avenues toward the palace of Taman. It was well, too, that we had a strong military escort, for the people who saw us pass thought that we were Zani prisoners; and would have made quick work of us had it not been for the soldiers. Even to the very gates of the palace of the jong they followed us, booing and cursing and flinging insults at us. The officer who escorted us tried to tell them that we were not Zanis, but his voice was drowned in the tumult.

127

XVII: Forty Minutes!

When word was taken to Taman that I had returned to Sanara, he had us brought to him at once. He had known the Toganja Zerka well in Amlot, and after he had listened to her story he promised that both she and Mantar should be rewarded for the hazardous work they had performed in the stronghold of the Zanis. Upon me he conferred nobility, promising me palaces and land also as soon as the seat of government should have been re-established in Amlot. When he learned of the attitude of the Sanarans toward us because of our Zani appearance, he ordered black wigs for Mantar and me and new apparel for all of us; then he turned Zerka and Mantar over to members of his household staff and took me to see Jahara, his queen. I knew that he wanted to talk to me in private and tell me about Duare, the one subject upper most in my mind but of which neither of us had spoken. The little Princess Nna was with her mother when we entered the apartments of the queen, and they both welcomed me with great cordiality and real friendship. Fortunately for Nna, she was not fettered by the ridiculous customs of Vepaja that had made of Duare a virtual prisoner in her own apartments in her father's palace; but could mingle as freely with the court as other members of the royal family. She was a sweet young girl and the pride of Taman and Jahara. Shortly after I was received by the latter, Nna was taken away by a lady-in-waiting; and I was not to see her again until after a harrowing episode and a dangerous adventure.

As soon as Taman, Jahara, and I were alone I turned to the former. "Tell me about Duare," I begged. "I saw the anotar leave Sanara this morning and head out over the ocean. No one but Duare could have been at the controls, for only she and I know how to fly the ship."

"You are right," he replied, "it was Duare."

"And she was flying her father back to Vepaja?" I asked.

"Yes. Mintep practically forced her to do so. She had not given up hope that you might be alive, and she wanted to remain. She was planning on flying back to Amlot with more bombs and a message that she would continue to bomb the city until you were released, but Mintep would not let her do so. He swore that if you did live, he would kill you on sight, for while, as a father, he owed you a debt of gratitude for all that you had done for his daughter, as Jong of Vepaja he must destroy you for having dared to love his daughter and take her as your mate. Finally he commanded her to return to Vepaja with him and stand trial before the nobles of Kooaad for having broken one of the oldest taboos of Vepaja."

"That may mean death for her," I said.

"Yes, she realized that; and so did Mintep, but the dynastic customs and laws of Vepaja are so ingrained in every fibre of their beings that, to them, it was almost unthinkable to attempt to evade them. Duare would have had she known that you lived. She told me that, and she also told me that she would return to Vepaja willingly because she preferred death to life without you. I do not know what Mintep would have done had she refused to return to Kooaad; but I think he would have killed her with his own hands, notwithstanding the fact that he loved her. I was, however, prepared for such an eventuality; and I should have protected Duare even to the extent of imprisoning Mintep. I can tell you that we were all in a most unhappy situation. I never before saw a man of such unquestioned intelligence so fanatical as Mintep, but on this one subject only. Otherwise he seemed perfectly normal and lavished upon Duare all the love of a devoted father. I have often wondered what he would have done if Duare had found you at Amlot. I can't imagine him in the anotar with you. But, tell me, what went wrong with your plans? Duare said that you did not put off from the city in a boat as you should have done were you released."

"I put off just as had been planned; but I had Zerka and Mantar with me, and Duare would have been looking for a lone man in a boat. Also, my flying helmet had been taken from me in the courtroom of the prison; so there was nothing by which she could identify me. We must have looked like three Zanis to her."

"Then she saw you," said Taman, "for she told me that she saw three Zanis put off into the harbor. When you did not come as she had hoped, she assumed that the Zanis had killed you; and she bombed the city until she had exhausted her supply of bombs. Then she flew back with Mintep, Ulan, and Legan; and remained in the vicinity of Sanara for several days until we sent up three balloons to indicate that it was safe for you to enter Sanara—of course, at that time, we did not know that you were not in the ship."

"And what of Muso? I was told at the gate that he had been deposed."

"Yes, and imprisoned," replied Taman; "but he has a number of followers whose lives will not be safe in Korva now that Muso is no longer jong. They are desperate. Last night they succeeded in liberating Muso from prison, and he is hiding now somewhere in the city. We do not believe that he has been able to leave Sanara as yet, though that is his plan. He believes that if he can reach Amlot, the Zanis will make him jong; but he does not know what we know—that Mephis is dead and that after his death the counterrevolutionists struck and completely routed the Zani overlords, of whom the people, including the majority who claimed to be Zanis, were heartily sick. The word must have reached the troops before Sanara yesterday morning, for it was then that they evacuated their positions and started on the long march back toward Amlot."

"Then the long civil war is over," I said.

"Yes," replied Taman, "and I hope soon to re-establish the capital at Amlot. I have already sent word that I would extend amnesty to all except ringleaders and those whose acts have been definitely criminal. I expect to follow my messenger in person in a few days with a powerful army. And, my friend, I hope that you will accompany me and receive in my capital the honors that are your due."

I shook my head. "Do not think that I don't appreciate your generosity," I said, "but I think you will understand that they would be empty honors indeed without my princess to share them."

"But why not?" he urged. "You must live, and here you may live in comfort and in honor. What other plans may you have?"

"I am going to follow Duare to Vepaja."

"Impossible!" he exclaimed. "How can you hope to reach Vepaja? Every Korvan vessel was taken or destroyed by the enemy during the last war."

"I have a boat that brought me safely from Amlot," I reminded him.

"What is it? a fishing boat?" he demanded.

"Yes."

"A mere cockleshell," he cried. "You would not last through the first storm."

"Nevertheless, I shall make the attempt," I said.

He shook his head sadly. "I wish that I might dissuade you," he said, "not alone because of my friendship for you, but because you could be of such great value to Korva."

"How?" I asked.

"By showing us how to build anotars and training my officers to fly them."

"The temptation is great," I admitted, "but I shall never rest in peace until I know that I have done all that man can do to rescue Duare."

"Well, you can't leave at once; so we shall make the most of the time that you are with us; and I shall not annoy you with further importunities."

He called an aide then, and had me shown to the quarters he had assigned me. There I found new apparel and a black wig; and after a hot bath I felt like a new man; and looked like one, too, as my mirror revealed in a startling manner. I should not have known myself, so greatly did the wig change my appearance.

Zerka, Mantar, and I dined that night in the great banquet hall of the jong's palace with Taman and Jahara and a company of the great nobles of Korva. They had all known me, some of them quite well; but they all agreed that they would never have recognized me. This, I realized, was not entirely due to the black wig. I had lost considerable weight during my hazardous adventures in Amlot; and I had undergone considerable mental suffering, with the result that my face was haggard and lined, my cheeks sunken.

During the long dinner, we three from Amlot fairly monopolized the conversation, but not through any desire on our part. The other guests insisted upon hearing every detail of what we had observed there and what we had experienced. They were especially interested in Zerka's description of the devious methods whereby the counterrevolutionists had carried on their operations despite the highly organized Zani spy system and the ruthless extermination of all who became suspected. They were still listening to her, spellbound, when a highly agitated aide entered the banquet hall and approached Taman. As he whispered in the jong's ear, I saw the latter turn suddenly pale; then he rose and, taking Jahara's hand, led her from the hall. While the jong's departure left us free to depart if we wished, no one did so. We all felt that Taman was in trouble, and I think that as one man our only thought was to remain, in the event that we might be of service to our jong. We were right, for presently the aide returned and asked us to remain until Taman could speak with us. A few moments later he returned to the banquet hall; and, standing at the head of the long table, spoke to us.

"In this hall," he said, "are many of my most loyal subjects and trusted friends. I have come to you in a moment of great trouble to ask your aid. The Janjong Nna has been abducted from the palace."

An involuntary exclamation of shock and sorrow filled the great room.

"She was taken with the connivance of someone in the palace," continued Taman, "but not before two loyal guardsmen had been killed attempting to defend her. That is all I know."

A voice murmured, "Muso!" It reflected the thought in every mind; and just then an officer hurried into the hall and up to Taman, handing him a message.

"This was just found in the janjong's apartment," said the officer.

Taman read the message through; then he looked up at us. "You were right," he said. "It was Muso. This is a threat to kill Nna unless I abdicate in favor of Muso and swear allegiance to him."

We all stood there voiceless. What was there to say? Could we advise a father to sacrifice a loved daughter? Could we permit Muso to become jong of Korva? We were upon the horns of a dilemma.

"Does the message state any time when your decision must be reached?" asked Varo, the general.

Taman nodded. "Between the first and second hours in the morning I must send up balloons from the palace roof—one, if I refuse; two, if I accede."

"It is now the 26th hour," said Varo. "We have eleven hours in which to work. In the meantime, Taman, I beg that you refrain from making any reply. Let us see what we can accomplish."

"I shall leave the matter in your hands, Varo," said Taman, "until the 1st hour tomorrow. Keep me advised of any progress, but please do not jeopardize the life of my daughter."

"Her safety shall be our first concern," Varo assured the jong.

Taman sat with us while we discussed plans. There seemed nothing more practical than a thorough search of the city, and Varo issued orders that routed out every soldier in Sanara to prosecute such a search as few cities ever have been subjected to.

I asked permission to join the searchers, and when Varo granted it I went at once to my quarters and summoned the servant who had been detailed to attend me. When he came I asked him if he could quickly procure for me the apparel such as a poor man might wear, but one who might also reasonably carry a sword and pistol.

"That will be easy, sir," he said. "I have only to go to my own quarters and fetch the apparel that I wear when I am not in the livery of the jong's household."

In ten minutes I was attired in the clothing of an ordinary citizen of the lower class, and was soon on the street. I had a plan—not a very brilliant one but the best I could think of. I knew some rather disreputable haunts of the underworld of Sanara where men might foregather who could be bribed to commit any crime however heinous, and it occurred to me that here I might overhear much discussion of a crime with which such men would be familiar and possibly a hint that would lead me on the right trail. I really didn't have much enthusiasm for the idea, but I had to do something. I liked little Nna, and I couldn't just sit still and do nothing while she was in danger.

I wandered down toward the lower end of the city where the fish markets had been and where the sailors had gathered to carouse and fight in the days before the war that had wiped out the merchant marine and most of the fishing industry of Sanara. Now it was almost deserted, but there were still many of the old drinking places eking out a mean existence by catering to the men and women of the underworld. I went from one to the other of them, buying drinks here, gambling there, and always listening for any chance scrap of conversation that might lead to a clue. There was much talk on the subject of the abduction of the princess, for the matter was uppermost in all minds; but nothing was said in any of the places I went right up to the 36th hour that would have indicated any knowledge of the whereabouts of Nna or of her abductors.

I was discouraged and about hopeless as the 36th hour saw me sitting in a dive near the river wall of Sanara, where I pretended to be slightly under the influence of the vile drink that is popular there and tastes something like a mixture of gin and kerosene oil, of neither of which am I very fond—as a beverage. I let myself be enticed into a gambling game that somewhat resembles fan-tan. I lost consistently and paid with great good humor.

"You must be a rich man," said an ugly looking customer seated beside me.

"I know how to make money," I said. "I have made a lot this night. I may hang for it; so I might as well spend it."

"That's the idea," he applauded. "But how did you make so much money so easily?"

"That I should tell—and get my neck twisted," I said.

"I'll bet I know how he made it," offered another man, "and he will get his neck twisted for it, too—unless—"

"Unless what?" I demanded truculently.

"You know and so do Prunt and Skrag. They've gone for the rest of theirs now."

"Oh, they have, have they?" I demanded. "I haven't got the rest of mine. I don't know where to go to get it. They'll probably cheat me out of it. Oh, well, I've got plenty anyway." I got up from the table and walked toward the door, staggering just a little. I hadn't the remotest idea that I was on a trail that would lead where I wanted to go, but there was a chance. This was probably the biggest crime that had been committed in Sanara since it was founded; and when a great deal of money was exhibited under the conditions and in the manner that I had exhibited mine, it would naturally suggest connection of some kind with the criminals, for a man of my apparent walk of life would not have come suddenly upon great wealth honestly.

I had scarcely reached the door of the dive when I felt a hand on my arm. I turned to look into the cunning face of the man who had spoken to me last. "Let us talk together, my friend," he said.

"What about?" I asked.

"You have some money coming to you," he commenced. "What would you give me if I should show you where you could collect it?"

"If you can do that, I might give you half," I said.

"Very well," he said, "for half I will do it. But this is a bad night to be about on work of this kind. Since they stole the jong's daughter the city is being searched and everyone being questioned. The boys got a lot of money for that. What you got for choking the old villain, Kurch, would be nothing beside what Muso paid to have the daughter of the jong brought to him."

So I was off on a wrong trail! But how to get on the right one? The fellow was obviously drunk, which accounted for his loose tongue; and he knew something about the abduction of Nna, but how much? And how was I to switch him from one trail to another? I saw that I would have to take the bull by the horns.

"What made you think I had anything to do with murdering Kurch?" I demanded.

"Didn't you?" he asked.

"Of course not," I assured him. "I never said I did."

"Then how did you come by so much money?" he demanded.

"Don't you suppose there were other jobs besides the Kurch job," I demanded.

"There were only two big jobs in town tonight," he said. "If you were in on the other, you ought to know where to go."

"Well, I don't," I admitted. "I think they're tryin' to beat me out of mine. They said they'd bring me the rest of mine down here, but they aren't here. They wouldn't tell me where they took the girl, either. I'd give anything to know. If I did, you can bet they'd come through, or—" I touched my sword significantly.

"How much would you give?" he asked.

"What difference does that make to you?" I demanded. "You don't know where she is."

"Oh, I don't, don't I? Just show me how high your money stacks. I know lots of things for a tall stack."

Korvan money is all of the same metal, round pieces of different thicknesses, their centers punched out with different size circles, squares, ovals, and crosses; but all of the same outside diameter. Their value is determined by the weight of the metal each contains. They stack easily, and the thicker pieces of greatest value naturally stack higher, giving usage to the common expression "a tall stack" meaning a considerable amount of money.

"Well, if you really showed me where she is," I said, "I might give you five hundred pandars." A pandar has about the purchasing power in Korva that a dollar would have in America.

"You haven't got that much," he said.

I shook my pocket pouch so that the money in it rattled. "Doesn't that sound like it?" I asked.

"I like to feel money, not listen to it," he said.

"Well, come outside where no one will see us; and I'll show it to you."

I saw the cunning glint in his eyes as we passed out into the avenue. Finding a spot that was deserted and also dimly lighted by a lamp in a window, I counted out five hundred pandars into his cupped palms, definitely defeating for the moment any plan he had to murder me; then, before he could transfer the money to his pocket pouch, I drew my pistol and shoved it into his belly.

"If there's any shooting to be done, I'll do it," I told him. "Now take me to where the girl is, and no funny business. When you have done that, you may keep the money; but if you make a single break, or fail to show me the girl, I'll let you have it. Get going."

He grinned a sickly grin, and turned away down the dark street. As he did so, I jerked his pistol from its holster; and shoved the muzzle of mine into the small of his back. I wasn't taking any chances.

"You're all right, fellow," he said. "When this job's over, I'd like to work with you. You work quick, and you know what you're doing. Nobody ain't going to fool you."

"Thanks," I said. "Be at the same place tomorrow night, and we'll talk it over." I thought this might keep him from trying to double-cross me, but I still kept my gun in his ribs.

He led me along the river wall to an old, abandoned building at one end of which was a huge incinerator within a firebox large enough to hold half a dozen men. He stopped here and listened, looking furtively in all directions.

"She's in here," he whispered. "This firebox opens into the inside of the building, too. Now give me back my pistol and let me go."

"Not so fast," I cautioned him. "The agreement was that you were to show me the girl. Go on in!"

He hesitated, and I prodded him with my gun.

"They'll kill me," he whimpered.

"If you don't show me the girl, they won't have to," I threatened. "Now don't talk any more—we may be overheard. If I have to go in alone, I'll leave you out here, dead."

He said no more, but he was shaking as he crawled into the great incinerator. I laid his pistol on the ledge of the firebox and followed directly behind him. It was dark as a pocket in the firebox and not much better in the room into which we stepped—so dark that I had to hold onto my companion's trappings to keep him from eluding me entirely. We stood in silence, listening for a full minute. I thought I heard the murmur of voices. My guide moved forward cautiously, feeling his way step by step. It was evident that he had been here before. He crossed to the side of the room, where he found a bolted door.

"This is for our getaway," he whispered, as he drew the bolt. I knew from the direction we had come that the door opened out onto the street.

He turned and moved diagonally across the room again to the opposite wall. Here he found another door which he opened with the utmost caution. When it was opened, the murmur of voices became more distinct. Ahead of us, I could see a tiny ray of dim light coming apparently from the floor of the room. My guide led me forward to it, and I saw that it came through a hole in the flooring—possibly a knothole.

"Look!" he whispered.

As I had to lie down on my stomach to look through the hole, I made him lie down, also. In the circumscribed range of my vision, I could not see much of the room below; but what I did see was almost enough. Two men were sitting at a table, talking—one of them was Muso. I could see no girl, but I knew that she might be there outside the little circle that was visible to me. I could hear the men talking.

"You don't really intend killing her, do you?" asked Muso's companion.

"If I don't get a favorable reply from Taman before the 2nd hour, I most certainly shall," replied Muso. "If she would write her father as I have asked her to, she would be free to go at once; for I know that Taman would not see his daughter die if she herself begged him to save her."

"You'd better do it, Nna," said the other man. "The time is getting short."

"Never!" said a girl's voice, and I knew that I had found Nna.

"You may go now," I whispered to my companion. "You will find your pistol on the ledge of the incinerator. But wait! How can I get into that room?"

"There is a trap door in the corner, to your right," he replied. He moved away so silently that I did not hear him go, but I knew that he had. Only a fool would have remained with me.

Faintly into the darkness of the room came a suggestion of growing light. The sun was rising. The first hour had come. In forty minutes of Earth time the second hour would strike—strike the death knell of Nna, the daughter of Taman.

XVIII: A TANJONG

Forty minutes! What could I do in that time to insure the safety of the princess? Had I found her only a little sooner, I could have summoned soldiers and surrounded the building. They would not have killed her had they known they were going to be taken. But I must do something. The precious minutes were slipping by. There was nothing for it but to take the bull by the horns and do the best I could. I rose and felt my way to the corner of the room. On hands and knees I groped about in the darkness for the trap door, and at last I found it. Gingerly I tried it to learn if it were locked from below. It was not. I raised it quickly and jumped through, my pistol still in my hand. I heard it slam shut above my head as I touched the floor. Luckily, I did not fall; and my advent had been so sudden and so unexpected that for an instant Muso and his companion seemed unable to move or speak. I backed to the wall and covered them.

"Don't move," I warned, "or I'll kill you both."

It was then that I first saw two men in the far corner of the dimly lighted room as they leaped to their feet from a pile of rags upon which they had been lying asleep. As they reached for their pistols I opened fire on them. Muso dropped to the floor behind the table at which he had been sitting, but his companion now drew his own weapon and levelled it at me. I shot him first. How all three of them could have missed me in that small room I cannot understand. Perhaps the brains of two of them were dulled by sleep, and the other was unquestionably nervous. I had seen his hand shake as it held his weapon; but miss me they did, and the second and third went down before they could find me with the deadly stream of r–rays from their guns. Only Muso remained. I ordered him out from under the table and took his pistol from him; then I looked about for Nna. She was sitting on a bench at the far side of the room.

"Have they harmed you in any way, Nna?" I asked.

"No; but who are you? Do you come from my father, the jong? Are you a friend or another enemy?"

"I am your friend," I said. "I have come to take you away from here and back to the palace." She did not recognize me in my black wig and mean apparel.

"Who are you?" demanded Muso, "and what are you going to do to me?"

"I am going to kill you, Muso," I said. "I have hoped for this chance, but never expected to get it."

"Why do you want to kill me? I haven't harmed the princess. I was only trying to frighten Taman into giving me back the throne that belongs to me."

"You lie, Muso," I said; "but it is not this thing alone that I am going to kill you for—not something that you may say you did not intend doing, but something you did."

"What did I ever do to you? I never saw you before."

"Oh, yes you have. You sent me to Amlot to my death, as you hoped; and you tried to steal my woman from me."

His eyes went wide and his jaw dropped. "Carson of Venus!" he gasped.

"Yes, Carson of Venus—who took your throne away from you and is now going to take your life, but not because of what you did to him. I could forgive that, Muso; but I can't forgive the suffering you caused my princess. It is for that that you are about to die."

"You wouldn't shoot me down in cold blood?" he cried.

"I should," I said, "but I am not going to. We'll fight with swords. Draw!"

I had laid his pistol on the bench beside Nna, and now I drew my own and placed it on the table at which Muso had been sitting; then we faced one another. Muso was no mean swordsman, and as our blades shattered the silence of that little room I commenced to suspect that I might have bitten off more than I could chew; so I fought warily and, I am free to admit, mostly on the defensive. That is no way to win any contest, but I knew that if I became too reckless in my attack he might easily slip cold steel through me. Yet something must be done. This could not go on like this forever. I redoubled my efforts; and because I had by now become accustomed to his mode of attack, which he seldom varied, I commenced to have the advantage. He realized it, too; and the yellow in him showed up immediately. Then I pressed my advantage. I backed him around the room, certain now that I could run him through almost at will. He stepped back against the table in what I took to be a last stand; then, suddenly, he hurled his sword directly in my face; and almost simultaneously I heard the br-r-r of an r-ray pistol. I had seen him reach for mine just as he hurled his sword at me. I expected to fall dead, but I did not. Instead, Muso slumped backward across the table and then rolled off onto the floor; and as I looked around, I saw Nna standing with Muso's pistol still leveled in her hand. She had robbed me of my revenge, but she had saved my life.

As I looked at her, she sat down very suddenly and burst into tears. She was just a little girl, and she had been through too much in the past few hours. She soon regained control of herself, however; and looked up and smiled at me, rather wanly.

"I really didn't know you," she said, "until Muso called you by name; then I knew that I was safe—that is, safer. We are not safe yet. His men were to return here at the 2nd hour. It must be almost that now."

"It is, and we must get out of here," I said. "Come!"

I slipped my pistol back into its holster; and we stepped to the ladder that led up to the trap door, and at the same moment we heard the heavy tramp of feet in the building above us. We were too late.

"They have come!" whispered Nna. "What are we to do?"

"Go back to your bench and sit down," I said. "I think one man may hold this doorway against many."

Stepping quickly to the sides of the dead men, I gathered their pistols and carried them all to a point from which I could command the ladder with the least danger to myself. The footsteps approached the room above us, they entered it and crossed to the trap door; and then a voice called down, "Hello, there, Muso!"

"What do you want of Muso?" I asked.

"I have a message for him."

"I will take it for him," I said. "Who are you? and what is your message?"

"I am Ulan, of the Jong's Guard. The message is from Taman. He agrees to your demands provided you will return Nna to him unharmed and guarantee the future safety of Taman and his family."

I breathed a sigh of relief and sat down in a nearby chair. "Muso scorns your offer," I said. "Come down, Ulan, and see for yourself why Muso is no longer interested."

"No trickery!" he warned, as he raised the trap door and descended. When he turned at the foot of the ladder and saw the four corpses lying on the floor his eyes went wide as he recognized one of them as Muso; then he saw Nna and crossed to her.

"You are not harmed, Janjong?" he asked.

"No," she replied. "But if it had not been for this man I should have been dead by now."

He turned to me. I could see that he recognized me no more than others had. "Who are you?" he asked.

"Don't you remember me?"

Nna giggled, and I had to laugh myself.

"What is so funny?" he demanded. Ulan flushed angrily.

"That you should so soon forget a good friend," I said.

"I never saw you before," he snapped, for he knew we were making fun of him.

"You never saw Carson of Venus?" I asked; then he laughed with us as he finally pierced my disguise. "But how did you know where to find the princess?"

"When Taman gave the required signal of acquiescence," explained Ulan, "one of Muso's agents told us where she might be found."

We were soon out of that dank cellar and on our way to the palace, where we brushed past the guards under escort of Ulan and hastened through the palace to the jong's own quarters. Here Taman and Jahara sat waiting for word from the last of the searchers or from the emissary the former had dispatched to Muso at the urgings of Jahara and his own heart. As the door was thrown open we sent Nna in, Ulan and I remaining in a small antechamber, knowing that they would wish to be alone. A jong would not wish his officers to see him weep, as I am sure Taman must have wept for joy at Nna's safe return.

It was but a few minutes before he came out into the antechamber. His face was grave by now. He looked somewhat surprised to see me, but he only nodded as he turned to Ulan.

"When will Muso return to the palace?" he asked.

We both looked at him in surprise. "Didn't the janjong tell you?" asked Ulan. "She must have told you."

"Tell me what? She was crying so for joy that she could not speak coherently. What is there to tell me, that I may not already guess?"

"Muso is dead," said Ulan. "You are still jong."

From Ulan, and later from Nna, he finally got the whole story, pieced out with what I told him of my search through the city; and I have seldom seen a man more grateful. But I expected that from Taman; so I was not surprised. He always gave fully of himself to his friends and his loyal retainers.

I thought I should sleep forever when I went to bed that morning in my apartments in the jong's palace, but they didn't let me sleep as long as I could have wished. At the 12th hour I was awakened by one of Taman's aides and summoned to the great throne room. Here I found the grand council of nobles assembled around a table at the foot of the throne and the rest of the room crowded with the aristocracy of Korva.

Taman and Jahara and Nna sat in their respective thrones upon the dais, and there was a fourth chair at Taman's left. The aide led me to the foot of the dais before Taman and asked me to kneel. I think Taman is the only man in two worlds before whom I should be proud to kneel. Above all other men, he deserves reverence for his qualities of mind and soul. And so I knelt.

"To save the life of my daughter," commenced Taman, "I offered my throne to Muso with the consent of the grand council. You, Carson of Venus, saved my daughter and my throne. It is the will of the grand council, in which I concur, that you be rewarded with the highest honor in the power of a jong of Korva to bestow. I therefore elevate you to the rank of royalty; and as I have no son, I adopt you as my own and confer upon you the title of Tanjong of Korva." Then he rose and, taking me by the hand, led me to the vacant throne chair at his left.

I had to make a speech then, but the less said about that the better—as a maker of speeches, I am a fairly good aviator. There were speeches by several great nobles, and then we all trooped to the banquet hall and overate for a couple of hours. This time I did not sit at the foot of the table. From a homeless wanderer a few months earlier, I had been suddenly elevated to the second position in the empire of Korva. But that was all of lesser moment to me than the fact that I had a home and real friends. If only my Duare had been there to share it all with me!

Here at last I had found a country where we might live in peace and honor, only to be thwarted by that same malign fate that had snatched Duare from my arms on so many other occasions.

XIX: PIRATES

I never really had an opportunity to more than taste the honors and responsibilities that devolve upon a crown prince, for the next day I started outfitting my little fishing boat for the long trip to Vepaja.

Taman tried to dissuade me, as did Jahara and Nna and all my now countless friends in Korva; but I could not be prevailed upon to abandon the venture, however hopeless I myself felt it to be. The very ease and luxury of my new position in life made it seem all the more urgent that I search for Duare, for to enjoy it without her seemed the height of disloyalty. I should have hated it always had I remained.

Every assistance was given me in outfitting my craft. Large water tanks were installed and a device for distilling fresh water from sea water. Concentrated foods, preserved foods, dehydrated fruits and vegetables, nuts, every edible thing that could be preserved for a considerable time were packed away in waterproof containers. New sails were made of the strong, light "spider cloth" that is common among the civilized countries of Amtor, where spiders are bred and kept for the purpose of spinning their webs for commercial use, as are silkworms on Earth. They gave me weapons and ammunition and warm blankets and the best navigation instruments available; so that I was as well equipped for the journey as it was possible for anyone to be.

At last the time of my departure arrived, and I was escorted to the river with all the pomp and ceremony befitting my exalted rank. There were troops and bands and a hundred gorgeously caparisoned gantors bearing not only the nobility of Korva but its royalty as well, for Taman and Jahara and the Princess Nna rode with me in the howdah of the jong's own gantor. Cheering throngs lined the avenues and it should have been a happy event, but it was not—not for me, at least; for I was leaving these good friends, as I full believed, forever and with little or no hope of attaining my heart's desire. I shall not dwell further upon the sadness of that leave-taking. The pall of it hung over me as I sailed out upon the broad expanse of that vast and lonely ocean, nor did my spirits lift until long after the distant mountains of Anlap had dropped below the horizon; then I shook the mood from me as I looked with eagerness toward the future and set my mind solely upon success.

I had set a range of from ten to twenty days for the cruise to Vepaja, depending, of course, upon the winds; but there was always the possibility of missing the island entirely, notwithstanding the fact that it was a continent in size, being some four thousand miles long by fifteen hundred wide at its greatest width. Such a supposition might seem ridiculous on Earth, but here conditions were vastly different. Maps were inaccurate. Those available indicated that Anlap was scarcely more than five hundred miles from Vepaja, but I knew that at least fifteen hundred miles of ocean must separate them. Duare and I had learned that when we had flown it. The reason their maps must be inaccurate is due to their false conception of the shape of the planet, which they believe to be a flat disc floating on a sea of molten rock, and their further belief that the antarctic region forms the periphery and what I knew to be the equator, the center of the disc. This naturally distorts every possible conception of the shape and size of oceans and land masses. These people in the southern hemisphere of Venus have not the remotest idea of the existence of the northern hemisphere.

I shall not inflict upon you the monotony of the first week of that journey. The wind held steady, and at night I lashed the tiller and slept with a comparatively peaceful mind, as I had devised an alarm that sounded whenever the boat deviated from its course a certain number of points. It was a simple device electrically controlled by the needle of the compass. I was not awakened on an average of two or three times in a night; so I felt that I was keeping fairly well on my course; but I wished that I knew what, if anything, the currents were doing to me.

Since the coast of Anlap had dropped below the horizon I had seen no land, nor had a single ship appeared upon that vast watery expanse of loneliness. The waters often teemed with fish; and occasionally I saw monstrous creatures of the deep, some of which defy description and would challenge belief. The most numerous of these larger creatures must attain a length of fully a thousand feet. It has a wide mouth and huge, protruding eyes between which a smaller eye is perched upon a cylindrical shaft some fifteen feet above its head. The shaft is erectile; and when the creature is at rest upon the surface or when it is swimming normally beneath, it reclines along its back; but when alarmed or searching for food, the shaft springs erect. It also functions as a periscope as the beast swims a few feet beneath the surface. The Amtorians call it a rotik, meaning three-eye. When I first saw one I thought it an enormous ocean liner as it lay on the surface of the ocean in the distance.

At dawn of the eighth day I saw the one thing that I could have wished least of all to see—a ship; for no ship that sailed the Amtorian seas could conceivably contain any friends of mine, unless, perhaps the Sofal was still carrying on its piratical trade with the crew that had followed me so loyally in the mutiny that had given me command of it. That, however, was doubtful. The vessel was some distance to starboard and was moving in an easterly direction. Within an hour it would cross my course, which was due south. Hoping to avoid detection because of the insignificant size of my little craft, I lowered my sails and drifted. For half an hour the ship held to its course; then its bow swung in my direction. I had been sighted.

It was a small vessel of about the tonnage of the Sofal, and very similar in appearance. It had no masts, sails, stacks, nor funnels. Aft were two oval deck houses, a small one resting on top of a larger. On top of the upper house was an oval tower surmounted by a small crow's nest. At bow and stern and from the crow's nest rose staffs from which long pennons flew. The main staff, above the crow's nest, was supposed to fly the flag of the country to which the ship belonged; the flag at the bow, the city from which it sailed; the stern flag was usually the house flag of the owner. In the case of warships, his staff carried the battle flag of the nation to which it belonged. As the ship neared me, I saw but one thing—a ship without country or city was a faltar, a pirate ship. The flag at the stern was probably the personal flag of the captain. Of all the disasters that could have befallen me, this was about the worst, that I should run foul of a pirate ship; but there was nothing to do about it. I could not escape. As I had thought it best to wear my black wig through the streets of Sanara on my way to the boat, I still had it with me; and as my yellow hair had only partially grown out and as I had a black-tipped mane reaching from forehead to nape, I put the wig on now rather than take the chance that my weird coiffure might arouse suspicion aboard the pirate craft.

As the ship came close, it lay to. I saw its name painted along the bow in the strange Amtorian characters—Nojo Ganja. Fully a hundred men lined the port rail watching me, as were several officers upon the upper decks of the houses. One of the latter hailed me.

"Come alongside," he shouted, "and come aboard."

It was not an invitation—it was a command. There was nothing to do but obey; so I raised one sail and brought my craft under the lee rail of the pirate. They tossed me a rope which I made fast to the bow and another with knots in it up which I climbed to the deck; then several of them slid down into my boat and passed every thing in it up to their fellows above. After that, they cut my boat adrift and got under way. All this I saw from an upper deck where I had been taken to be questioned by the captain.

"Who are you?" he asked.

"I am called Sofal," I said. Sofal was the name of my pirate ship and means "the killer."

"Sofal!" he repeated, a little ironically I thought. "And from what country do you hail? and what are you doing out here in the middle of the ocean in a small boat like that?"

"I have no country," I replied. "My father was a faltargan, and I was born on a faltar." I was rapidly becoming a proficient liar, I who had always prided myself on my veracity; but I think a man is sometimes justified in lying, especially if it saves a life. Now the word faltargan has an involved derivation. *Faltar*, pirate ship, derives from *ganfal*, criminal (which is derived from *gan*, man, and *fal*, kill) and *notar*, ship—roughly criminal ship. Add *gan*, man, to *faltar*, and you have pirate-ship-man, or pirate; fal-tär'gän.

"And so I suppose you are a pirate," he said, "and that that thing down there is your faltar."

"No," I said, "and yes; but, rather, yes and no."

"What are you driving at?" he demanded.

"Yes, I am a pirate; but no, that is not a faltar. It is just a fishing boat. I am surprised that an old sailor should have thought it a pirate ship."

"You have a loose tongue, fellow," he snapped.

"And you have a loose head," I retorted; "that is why you need a man like me as one of your officers. I have captained my own faltar, and I know my trade. From what I have seen, you haven't enough officers to handle a bunch of cut-throats such as I saw on deck. What do you say?"

"I say you ought to be thrown overboard," he growled. "Go to the deck and report to Folar. Tell him I said to put you to work. An officer! Cut out my liver! but you have got nerve! If you make a good sailor, I'll let you live. That's the best you'll get, though. Loose head!" and I could hear him grumbling as I went down the companionway to the deck.

I don't know just why I had deliberately tried to antagonize him, unless it was that I had felt that if I cringed before him he would have been more likely to have felt contempt for me and killed me. I was not unfamiliar with men of his type. If you stand up to them they respect and, perhaps, fear you, for most swashbucklers are, at heart, yellow.

When I reached the deck I had an opportunity to inspect my fellow sailors more closely. They were certainly a prize aggregation of villainous-looking scoundrels. They eyed me with suspicion and dislike and not a little contempt, as they appraised my rich apparel and handsome weapons which seemed to them to bespeak the dandy rather than the fighting man.

"Where is Folar?" I asked of the first group I approached.

"There, ortij oolja," he replied in an assumed falsetto, as he pointed to a huge bear of a man who was glowering at me a few yards away.

Those within earshot guffawed at this witticism—ortij oolja means *my love*. Evidently they thought my apparel effeminate. I had to smile a little myself, as I walked over to Folar.

"The captain told me to report to you for duty," I said.

"What's your name?" he demanded, "and what do you think you can do aboard a ship like the Nojo Ganja?"

"My name is Sofal," I replied, "and I can do anything aboard ship or ashore that you can do, and do it better."

"Ho! ho!" he pretended to laugh, "The Killer! Listen, brothers, here is The Killer, and he can do anything better than I can!"

"Let's see him kill you, then," cried a voice from behind him.

Folar wheeled about. "Who said that?" he demanded, but nobody answered.

Again a voice from behind him said, "You're afraid of him, you sailful of wind." It seemed to me that Folar was not popular. He completely lost his temper then, over which he appeared to have no control whatsoever; and whipped out his sword. Without giving me an opportunity to draw, he swung a vicious cut at me that would have decapitated me had it connected. I leaped back in time to avoid it; and before he could recover, I had drawn my own weapon; then we settled down to business, as the men formed a circle around us. As we measured one another's strength and skill in the first few moments of the encounter, I heard such remarks as, "Folar will cut the fool to pieces," "He hasn't a chance against Folar—I wish he had," and "Kill the mistal, fellow; we're for you."

Folar was no swordsman; he should have been a butcher. He swung terrific cuts that would have killed a gantor, could he have landed; but he couldn't land, and he telegraphed his every move. I knew what he was going to do before he started to do it. Every time he cut, he left himself wide open. I could have killed him any one of half a dozen times in the first three minutes of our duel, but I didn't wish to kill him. For all I knew he might be a favorite of the captain, and I had already done enough to antagonize that worthy. For the right moment to do the thing I wanted to do, I had to bide my time. He rushed me about here and there dodging his terrific swings until, at last, I got tired of it and pricked him in the shoulder. He bellowed like a bull at that; and, seizing his sword with both hands, came at me like a charging gantor. Then I pricked him again; and after that he went more warily, for I guess he had commenced to realize that I could kill him if I wished. Now he gave me the opportunity I had been awaiting, and in an instant I had disarmed him. As his weapon clattered to the deck, I stepped in, my point at his heart.

"Shall I kill him?" I asked.

"Yes!" rose in a thunderous chorus from the excited sailors.

I dropped my point. "No, I shall not kill him this time," I said. "Now pick up your sword, Folar; and we'll call everything square. What do you say?"

He mumbled something as he stooped to retrieve his weapon; then he spoke to a one-eyed giant standing in the front row of spectators.

"This fellow will be in your watch, Nurn," he said. "See that he works." With that, he quit the deck.

The men gathered around me. "Why didn't you kill him?" asked one.

"And have the captain order me thrown overboard?" I demanded. "No. I can use my brains as well as my sword."

"Well," said Nurn, "there was at least a chance that he wouldn't have; but there is no chance that Folar won't stab you in the back the first chance he gets."

My duel with Folar had established me in the good graces of the crew; and when they found that I could speak the language of the sea and of the pirate ship, they accepted me as one of them. Nurn seemed to take a special fancy to me. I think it was because he hoped to inherit Folar's rank in the event the latter were killed, for several times he suggested that I pick another quarrel with Folar and kill him.

While talking with Nurn I asked him where the Nojo Ganja was bound.

"We're trying to find Vepaja," he said. "We've been trying to find it for a year."

"Why do you want to find it?" I asked.

"We're looking for a man the Thorists want," he said. "They've offered a million pandars to anyone who'll bring him to Kapdor alive."

"Are you Thorists?" I asked. The Thorists are members of a revolutionary political party that conquered the former empire of Vepaja which once spread over a considerable portion of the south temperate zone of Amtor. They are the bitter enemies of Mintep as well as of all countries that have not fallen into their hands.

"No," replied Nurn, "we are not Thorists; but we could use a million pandars of anybody's money."

"Who is this Vepajan they want so badly?" I asked. I assumed that it was Mintep.

"Oh, a fellow who killed one of their ongyans in Kapdor. His name is Carson."

So! The long arm of Thora had reached out after me. I was already in the clutches of its fingers; but, happily for me, I was the only one who knew it. However, I realized that I must escape from the Nojo Ganja before it touched at any Thoran port.

"How do you know this Carson is in Vepaja?" I asked.

"We don't know," replied Nurn. "He escaped from Kapdor with the janjong of Vepaja. If they are alive, it is reasonable to believe they are in Vepaja; that, of course, is where he would have taken the janjong. We are going to search Vepaja first. If he isn't there, we'll go back to Noobol and search inland."

"I should think that would be quite a man-size job," I remarked.

"Yes, it will," he admitted, "but he should be an easy man to trace. Here and there inland someone must have seen him, and if anyone once saw this Carson they'd never forget him. He has yellow hair, and as far as anyone ever heard no one else in the world has yellow hair." I was grateful for my black wig. I hoped it was on securely.

"How are you going to get into the tree cities of Vepaja?" I asked. "They don't care much for strangers there, you know."

"What do you know about it?" he demanded.

"I've been there. I lived in Kooaad."

"You did? That's just where we expect to find Carson."

"Then maybe I can help," I suggested.

"I'll tell the captain. No one aboard has ever been to Kooaad."

"But how do you expect to get into that city? You haven't told me that. It's going to be very difficult."

"They'll probably let one man go in to trade," he said. "You see, we've picked up a lot of jewels and ornaments off the ships we've taken. A man could go in with some of these and if he kept his ears and eyes open, he'd soon find out whether or not Carson was there. If he is, we'll have to find some way to entice him aboard the Nojo Ganja."

"That should be easy," I said.

Nurn shook his head. "I don't know about that," he said.

"It would be easy for me, knowing Kooaad as I do," I said. "You see I have friends there."

"Well, first we've got to find Vepaja," he remarked quite aptly.

"That's easy, too," I told him.

"How so?"

"Go tell the captain that I can pilot him to Vepaja," I said.

"You really can?"

"Well, I think I can. One never knows, what with the rotten maps we have."

"I'll go now and talk with the captain," he said. "You wait here and, say, keep a weather eye open for Folar—he's the stinkingest mistal of all the stinking mistals on Amtor. Just keep your back against something solid and your eyes open."

XX: To Kooaad

I watched Nurn as he crossed the deck and ascended the companionway leading to the captain's quarters. If the captain could be persuaded to trust me, here was such an opportunity to enter Kooaad as might never come to me again. I knew from the course that the Nojo Ganja was holding that she was paralleling the coast of Vepaja, but too far off shore for the land to be visible. At least I was confident that such was true. I really could not know it, as one could know nothing for certain about his position on one of these Amtorian seas unless he were in sight of land.

As I stood by the rail waiting for Nurn to return, I saw Folar come on deck. His expression was black as a thunder cloud. He came directly toward me. A man near me said, "Look out, fellow! He's going to kill you." Then I saw that Folar carried one hand behind him and that his pistol holster was empty. I didn't wait then to see what he was going to do or when he was going to do it. I knew. I whipped out my own gun just as he raised his. We fired simultaneously. I could feel the r-rays pinging past my ear; then I saw Folar slump to the deck. Instantly a crowd surrounded me.

"You'll go overboard for this," said a man.

"It won't be as easy as that," said another, "but in the end you'll go overboard."

An officer who had witnessed the affair came running down from the upper deck house. He pushed his way through the crowd of sailors to me.

"So you're trying to live up to your name, are you, fellow?" he demanded.

"Folar was trying to kill him," spoke a sailor.

"And after he'd spared Folar's life," said another.

"Folar had a right to kill any member of the crew he wanted to kill," snapped the officer. "You mistals know that as well as I do. Take this fellow up to the captain and throw Folar overboard."

So I was taken up to the captain's quarters. He was still talking with Nurn as I entered. "Here he is now," said Nurn.

"Come in," said the captain, rather decently; "I want to talk with you."

The officer who had accompanied me looked rather surprised at the captain's seemingly friendly manner. "This man has just killed Folar," he blurted.

Nurn and the captain looked at me in astonishment. "What difference does it make?" I asked. "He wasn't any good to you, anyway, and he was just about to kill the only man who can pilot you to Vepaja and get into the city of Kooaad for you. You ought to thank me for killing him."

The captain looked up at the officer. "Why did he kill him?" he asked.

The officer told the story quite fairly, I thought; and the captain listened without comment until he had concluded; then he shrugged.

"Folar," he said, "was a mistal. Someone should have killed him long ago. You may go," he said to the officer and the sailors who had brought me up; "I want to talk with this man." When they had left, he turned to me. "Nurn says that you can pilot this ship to Vepaja and that you are acquainted in Kooaad. Is that right?"

"I am well acquainted in Kooaad," I replied, "and I believe I can pilot the Nojo Ganja to Vepaja. You will have to help me get into Kooaad, though. I'll be all right after I get in."

"What course shall we take?" he asked.

"What is your course now?"

"Due east," he replied.

"Change it to south."

He shook his head, but he gave the necessary orders. I could see that he was very skeptical of our chances of reaching Vepaja on the new course. "How long before we'll raise land?" he asked.

"That, I can't tell," I said; "but I'd keep a sharp lookout, and at night cut your speed down."

He dismissed me then, telling me that I'd be quartered with the officers. I found my new companions little different from the common sailors. They were all bravos and rascals; and, without exception, had been common sailors themselves. I found little in common with them, and spent most of my time in the crow's nest with the lookout watching for land.

It was right after the 1st hour the next morning that I discerned the black-appearing mass ahead that I knew to be the giant forest of Vepaja, those mighty trees that rear their heads five and six thousand feet to drink sustenance from the moisture of the inner cloud envelope that surrounds the planet. Somewhere in that black mass and a thousand feet above the ground was the great tree city of Kooaad. There, too, if she still lived, would be my Duare.

I went down to the captain's quarters myself to report sighting land, and as I reached the door I heard voices. I would not have stopped to listen; but the first word I heard was the name they knew me by, Sofal. The captain was speaking to one of his officers.

"—and when we are through with him, see that he's put out of the way. Let the men know that it was because he killed Folar. We can't let them think they can get away with anything like that. If I hadn't needed him, I'd have had him killed yesterday."

I walked away as noiselessly as I could; and returned a moment later, whistling. When I had reported land, they both came out. It was plainly visible by now, and shortly after the 2nd hour we were close in shore. We were a little too far east; so we came about and skirted the coast until I sighted the harbor. In the meantime I had suggested to the captain that he'd better lower his pirate flags and fly something more in keeping with his purportedly peaceful designs.

"What country are they friendly with?" he asked. "What far country, whose ships and men they might not be expected to recognize."

"I am quite sure that a ship from Korva would be welcomed," I told him; so the Korvan flag was run up at the bow and above the deck houses; while, for an owner's flag at the stern, he used one he had taken from a ship he had sunk. There was already a ship in the harbor, a vessel from one of the little islands that lie west of Vepaja. It was loading up with tarel. There was a strong company of Vepajan warriors on guard, for the port is quite some distance from Kooaad; and there is always danger of attack by Thorists or other enemies.

The captain sent me ashore to negotiate for entry into Kooaad as well as to assure the Vepajans that we were there on a friendly mission. I found the company in charge of two officers, both of whom I had known when I lived in Kooaad. One was Tofar, who had been captain of the palace guard and high in the confidence of Mintep; the other was Olthar, brother of my best friend in Kooaad, Kamlot. I fairly shook in my boots as I recognized them, for I did not see how it could be possible that they should fail to know me. However, as I stepped from the small-boat, I walked boldly toward them. They looked me straight in the face without a sign of recognition.

"What do you want in Vepaja?" they asked, their tones none too friendly.

"We are trading with friendly countries," I said. "We are from Korva."

"Korva!" they both exclaimed. "We had heard that the merchant marine of Korva had been destroyed in the last war."

"Practically all of it," I said. "A few ships escaped because they were on long cruises and knew nothing of the war until it was over. Our ship was one of these."

"What have you to trade?" asked Tofar.

"Ornaments and jewels, principally," I replied. "I should like to take them into one of your big cities. I think the ladies of the jong's palace would like to see them."

He asked me if I had any with me; and when I showed him some that I had brought along in my pocket pouch, he was much interested; and desired to see more. I did not want to take him aboard the Nojo Ganja for fear his suspicions might be aroused by the ruffianly appearance of the officers and crew.

"When do you go back to the city?" I asked.

"We leave here as soon as they finish loading that ship," he replied. "That should be within the hour; then we leave immediately for Kooaad."

"I'll get all my articles," I told him, "and go to Kooaad with you."

Olthar seemed rather taken aback by this, and looked questioningly at Tofar. "Oh, I think it will be all right," said the latter. "After all, he's only one man; and anyway he's from Korva—that will make a difference with Mintep. He and the janjong were well treated there. I have heard him speak in the highest terms of the jong of Korva and the nobles he met there."

I had difficulty in hiding my relief at this evidence that Duare was alive and in Kooaad. But was she alive? She had evidently reached Vepaja with her father, but she might already have been destroyed for having broken the taboo custom had laid upon her as janjong of Vepaja.

"You mention a janjong," I said. "I am glad to know that your jong has a daughter. He will wish to buy some of my jewels for her."

They made no reply, but I saw them exchange a quick glance.

"Go and get your stuff," Tofar said, "and we'll take you with us when we return to Kooaad."

The captain was delighted when he found what excellent progress I had made. "Try to persuade the man Carson to return to the ship with you, if you find he is in Kooaad," he said.

"I shall certainly find him in Kooaad," I told him. "I am sure of that."

A half hour later I set out with Tofar, Olthar, and their company through the great forest toward Kooaad. We had not gone far when Olthar told me that I should have to be blind-folded, and after that a soldier walked on either side of me to guide me and keep me from stumbling over obstacles. Knowing as I did how jealously the Vepajans have to guard the secret entrances to their tree cities I was not at all surprised at this precaution, but I may say that it made most awkward travelling. At last, however, we reached a spot where I was conducted through a doorway; and after the door was closed, the bandage was removed from my eyes. I found myself in the hollow interior of a great tree, standing in a cage with Tofar, Olthar, and some of the warriors. The others waited on the ground beside the cage. A signal was given, and the cage started to rise. For a thousand feet we were hoisted by a great windlass to the street level of Kooaad. Once again I stood on the highflung walkways of the first Amtorian city I had ever seen. Somewhere near me was Duare, if she still lived. I could feel my heart throb from the excitement of the moment.

"Take me to the palace," I said to Tofar. "I should like to get permission to show these beautiful things to the women of the jong's retinue."

"Come," he said, "I'll see if we can get permission."

A short walk brought us to the enormous tree from the interior of which the rooms of the palace of Mintep are carved. How familiar it all was! How it recalled my first days on Venus, and that day of days that I had first seen Duare and first loved her. Now I was coming again to the palace of her father, but with a price upon my head.

At the entrance to the palace was the familiar guard. I knew the captain of it well, but he did not recognize me. When Tofar stated my request, the captain entered the palace, telling us to wait. He was gone for some time, but when he returned he said that Mintep would be glad to welcome a Korvan merchant to his palace.

"He has sent word to the women that you will show your wares in the reception room inside the entrance," said the captain. "They will be gathering there soon; so you might as well come in."

"I'll leave him with you, then," said Tofar.

I reached into my package and selected a jeweled ring, which I proffered to Tofar. "Please accept this for your kindness to me," I said, "and take it to your woman with my compliments."

If he had only known that Carson Napier—Carson of Venus—was the donor!

The women of the palace gathered in the reception room, and I spread my jewels and ornaments out before them. I had known many of them and most of the men who came with them or followed them in to see what I had to offer, but not a one knew me.

There was one particularly lovely girl whom I knew to have been very close to Duare, one of her ladies-in-waiting, in fact; and her I sought to draw into conversation. She was much interested in one piece, but said that she could not afford to buy anything so expensive.

"But your man," I said. "Certainly he will buy it for you."

"I have no man," she said. "I serve the janjong, and I may have no man until she takes one; or until she dies." Her voice broke with a sob.

"Take it," I whispered. "I have sold many already. I can easily spare this piece; then, when I come again, if you can, you may pay me."

"Oh, but I couldn't do that," she cried, a little startled.

"Please," I begged. "It will make me very happy to know that this lovely piece, which I myself so much admire, has a setting worthy of its beauty."

I could see that she wanted it very badly, and when a woman wants a piece of jewelry or apparel, she will stop at little to possess it.

"Well," she said, after a pause, during which she fondled and admired the bauble, "I suppose I might pay you some time; and if I couldn't, I could give it back to you."

"I am glad that you have decided to keep it," I said. "I have another piece here that I should like very much to show to the janjong. Do you suppose it would be possible?"

"Oh, no," she said. "That would be quite impossible; and anyway, she—she—" Again her voice broke.

"She is in trouble?" I asked.

She nodded. "She is going to die!" She spoke in an awed whisper.

"Die?" I asked. "Why?"

"The council of nobles has so decreed."

"You love her?"

"Yes, of course. I would give my life for her."

"Do you mean that?" I demanded.

She looked at me in surprise. I had let my emotions get the better of my caution.

"Why do you take such an interest?" she asked.

156

I looked at her for a full minute, I guess, trying to read her soul through her eyes. I could see nothing in them but truth and sincerity and love—love for my Duare.

"I am going to tell you why," I said. "I am going to trust you. I am going to put my life in your hands and the life of your janjong as well. I am Carson Napier—Carson of Venus."

Her eyes went wide and she caught her breath. She looked at me for a long time. "Yes," she said, "I see now; but you have changed so."

"Suffering and a black wig make a big change in one's appearance," I said. "I have come here to save Duare. Will you help me?"

"I told you once I would give my life for her," she said. "That was no idle speech. What do you want me to do?"

"I want you to get me into Duare's quarters in some way and hide me there. That is all I ask of you."

She thought for a moment. "I have a plan," she said, presently. "Gather up your things and prepare to leave. Say that you will return tomorrow."

I did as she bid, making several sales at the same time. I told the purchasers that I would take payment when I came back the next day. I almost smiled when I thought of the rage of the pirate captain could he have known that I was giving his treasure away. When I had at last gathered up what remained, I started toward the door. Then Vejara, the lady-in-waiting, spoke to me in a voice that all might hear.

"Before you go," she said, "I wish that you would bring your things to the anteroom of my apartments. I have a piece of jewelry which I should like to match if possible. I think I saw something of yours that would answer."

"Thank you," I said, "I'll come with you now;" so we walked out of the reception room, and she led me along corridors to a door which she opened with a key, after glancing quickly around to see if we had been observed. "Quick!" she whispered. "In here. These are the apartments of the janjong. She is alone. I have done all that I can. Goodby and good luck!"

She closed the door after me and locked it. I found myself in a very small waiting room, empty but for two long benches, one on either side. Later I learned that it was where servants waited to be interviewed by the janjong. I crossed to a door at the opposite end and opened it quietly. Before me was a beautifully furnished apartment. On a divan, reading, was a woman. It was Duare. I entered the room, and as I did so she turned and looked at me. Her eyes went wide with incredulity as she sprang to her feet and faced me; then she ran and threw herself into my arms. Of all, she alone had known me!

157

Neither of us could speak for a full minute; and then, though there was so much to say, I would not let her speak of but one thing, nor would I—a plan of escape.

"It will be simple, now that you are here," she said. "The council of nobles has condemned me to die. I suppose they could do nothing else. They do not wish my death. They are all my friends, but the laws that govern the jongs of Vepaja are stronger than friendship or their love for me or anything in the world—except my love for you and yours for me. They will be glad if I escape, for they have done their duty. My father will be glad, too."

"But not the jong of Vepaja," I said.

"I think he will be a little glad also," she said.

"Why couldn't you have escaped without me, if it is so easy to escape?" I asked.

"Because I have given my word not to violate my arrest," she replied. "But I cannot help it if someone takes me by force."

She was very serious, and so I did not smile—outwardly. Duare is very sweet.

We talked then and planned until after dark. When her food was brought, she hid me; and then she shared it with me. We waited until the city had quieted down; then she came close to me. "You will have to carry me out of my quarters," she said, "for I may not go of my own free will."

In the palace there is a secret shaft down the interior of the great tree to the ground. There is no lift there—only a very long and tiresome climb down a ladder. It was never intended to be used except in emergencies of life and death, and only the jong and his family know of its existence. Down this we clambered. I thought that we should never reach the ground, but at last we did.

Duare had told me that she had fastened the ship down not far from this tree, which is close to the edge of the forest. If it were still there, and unharmed, our escape would be assured. If it were not, we were lost. That was a chance we had to take, for Duare was to have died on the morrow. There was no time for me to investigate.

Leaving the base of the tree we groped our way through the darkness, constantly fearful of attack by one of the terrible beasts that roam the Vepajan forest. When I finally thought that we must have missed the anotar in the darkness, or that it had been taken away, I saw it looming in front of us; and I am not ashamed to admit that tears came to my eyes as I realized that my Duare was safe at last—safe and with me.

A few minutes later we zoomed into the Amtorian sky; and, leveling off, turned the nose of the ship out over the grey Amtorian sea toward the northwest and the kingdom of Korva—our kingdom. Toward peace and happiness and friends and love.